LORD OF SHADOWS

A DARK RH ROMANCE PETER PAN RETELLING

BRUTAL NEVER BOYS 2

MONA BLACK

LORD OF SHADOWS
BRUTAL NEVER BOYS 2

After escaping Neverland and its mad lords, who in their right mind would ever wish to go back?

My memories from the island torment me. I am worried about Peter, Jas, and the other Lost Boys, no matter how badly I want to deny it. Coming back to my own world hasn't given me the relief I'd expected.

I miss them.

I miss what we did together.

I miss being with these men who understand me, understand what I need and give it to me, no questions asked, no regrets, no shame.

Leaving them, I was aware I might be signing their death warrant, but I was selfish. I thought I was happy in the human world.

But the truth is, I don't think I am. The only place I've ever felt safe and content and right in my own skin was with them, on the island. In Neverland.

So when Peter Pan appears below my window, I jump at the chance to go back.

Call me crazy.

I must be.

Will things be like before? Will I be able to help them? Will I face my fears? What about my feelings for them?

And their feelings for me?

NOTE: this book is the second one in a trilogy ending in a cliffy. It features mature situations with some dark themes and adult language. Warning for dubcon, blood, gun, & knife play, self-harm, violence, kidnapping, stalking, forced proximity, bondage, light BDSM, unhinged psycho men and M/M relationships. Also child abuse (past, off page) and rape involving the mains (past, off page). Only for +18 audiences.

The trilogy has been written and all three books will be released by June.

No AI was used in the creation of this book.

PART I

"Never say goodbye—because goodbye means going away and
going away means forgetting."
— J.M. Barrie, Peter Pan

1

PETER

I find myself staggering down the main street of town, feeling sick as a dog.

Truth is, I arrived here sick. Shaking with cravings. A junkie's son, a junkie myself, hooked on fucking fairydust.

Ah, you didn't know. Or you forgot.

Wendy doesn't know, either.

She doesn't know it was the only goddamn way for me to survive Neverland.

Weak, you might say. *Cowardly of you, Peter.* The Twins certainly said so, more than once. But they share a shadow that is whole. Mine is feral and torn, tugging on the wound. The pain is getting worse every day.

And leaving it behind to come to the human world hurts even worse.

Turning onto her street—Wendy's street—I make a beeline for the store entrance where I have my lair, where I have kept watch over her for all this time waiting for her to turn of age.

Waiting for her to show a sign of her power.

But like with every other Wendy, it didn't happen. I watched her life from afar, savoring every gesture, every expression on her pretty face, fantasizing about her being the one and convincing myself it would come, if only I was patient.

As time passed, I realized she needed protection I couldn't offer, not if I didn't want to interfere with the path of her fate. And yet I couldn't help myself.

The thought she wasn't the one damn near killed me.

By the time she turned eighteen, I knew I should give up. I wasn't going to take her to Neverland and watch her go mad. And yet I couldn't do it. Couldn't stop looking for her.

Then I grabbed her when she was in danger of dying, my patience snapping, my fear of losing her tearing through me like a blade, and took her with me, to the island.

So much for waiting. So much for giving up.

Tink was right.

I remember the other Wendies. Over the centuries, their faces blurred together, their reactions, their pasts, their doubts. But this one... this one hooked me from the start, worse than fairydust. I watched her grow up since she was a chubby little toddler, with her family in a little house on the coast. I watched her trials and tribulations. I watched her grow into a beautiful, strong woman.

A broken one.

Of all the Wendies born in the world, only a handful have called to me across the Veil between worlds. The ones who need me. The ones with nightmares.

The ones who might save us.

And yeah, in Neverland my memory may be going, but here, I remember everything—who I am, why all that shit went down, why this is important.

Why she is important.

And about the others, left in Neverland without me. Not that I can stay here long. Not while the spell lasts and my shadow belongs to Neverland. With every trip, it tears a little bit more, grows a little bit crazier, beastlier. It detaches from me even more.

This is probably my last trip to the human world while keeping my sanity.

As much as is left of it.

"Are you dying?" she'd asked me.

Yeah. All of us are, on the island. Our period of Grace is coming to an end. Failure is a hot bullet lodged in my chest. It's true, I brought them together, called them to arms, told them we could make a difference.

But in the end, I will take them all down with me.

Mea culpa.

Sliding down the wall, I park my ass on the piece of cardboard I placed there months ago, when I moved my watch closer to her apartment. I'd checked on her more periodically over the years as she grew up. I mean, a child wouldn't do. She'd called to me but I couldn't be sure. She had to be an adult woman for her magic to manifest.

Still waiting for that part. The magic. I mean, apart from the island changing, which may or may not be her doing.

And she doesn't believe me.

Doesn't care what happens to me.

To the others.

To Neverland.

To be fair, that place is made from her nightmares and traumas. Why would she wanna save it, right? Save us?

Right.

Problem, right there. One I cannot solve. It sucks to be rational and clear-thinking in the human world. To realize that I behave like a madman on the island. It feels as if it's someone else doing all that shit and yet I know it's me.

Clasping in my hand the small silver thimble that belongs to her, I hunker down as an icy wind blows. Snow threads the air. My stomach growls with hunger. And if she saved us? If she managed it? What then?

What would happen to us? We discussed it a few times, drunk, sitting on the beach of the island with the mermaids snapping at us. Would I return to the human world? Would one of the Twins? Would it be possible?

What about the Fae among us? What about the other Twin? What about Tink?

What about *Hook*?

Hook... Christ, *fuck*, what a mess. What happens when you don't have a shadow anymore? A human without a shadow. Not even a shred of your own soul to clutch to yourself. Feeling your mind unravel while a foreign, alien shadow digs its claws into you.

That's Hook.

And would that happen to Tink if he crossed over here? I've often wondered how Tink survived among humans before crossing to Neverland. How any visiting Fae survives. But maybe it's only a question of time, of how long you spend in the other dimension.

Probably why my own shadow is changing, pulling free. I've been in Neverland way too fucking long...

———

TIME PASSES WITH LURCHING LEAPS AS I DOZE ON AND OFF IN MY corner. I need to talk to Wendy, so I lurk like a perv, keeping an eye out for her.

Except my body is weakened by the pain and hunger and the cravings. All I have is my knives, and I already used them earlier to carve two lines on my arms.

Countering pain with pain, despair with destruction.

That's my way. The only way I know.

Fuck, I hurt. It's not only my shadow, not only the cravings, not just this fucked-up world, but also my link to the others. To the Island. I have to go back.

But what's the use of going back without Wendy?

She's not the one, I tell myself for the millionth time. *She's not the one, dammit, Peter. Let go.*

It almost sounds like Tink's voice in my head, and fuck, the thought of them suffering while I'm away does my head in.

The thought of all three of them suffering and Hook probably gloating nearby, getting a promotion in the Fae ranks, though I never understood why he's doing what he's doing, which only shows what a goddamn idiot I am—

"Wendy," I breathe, dragging myself to my feet.

She's coming down the street, dressed in black jeans and an overlong sweater, a jacket thrown over it. She's talking animatedly with her roommate, and I feel a stab of guilt for wanting to take her away from this easy, happy life, to wipe away this soft, pretty smile I never really got to see since I carried her off to Neverland.

Then I smell her scent of roses and my need for her rises, and as she steps closer, I remind myself that the nightmares making up the island are hers. She's no innocent bystander. She's involved in this.

In *us*.

So, I step in her way.

2

WENDY

"Don't look," Charlie says, "but I think it's that weirdo junkie again."

"Weirdo?" I glance toward the spot where he usually sits but can't see him. "Are we talking about the one who saved me from being mugged and maybe murdered?"

"*You* said he saved you." Charlie shrugs. "But you came home alone, and were confused and out of it. Can you swear it was him?"

I open my mouth to say yes and hesitate. My memory is foggy.

"Never mind, let's go." She tugs on my arm. "Our TV show is about to start."

"You know I don't care about tragic love stories, Charlie."

"But you'll watch it with me, won't you?" She pouts, bats her lashes. "And eat sweet popcorn?"

"I'm not sure," I start and stop, stumbling over my feet.

The junkie steps in our way, looming over us. He's a good six feet four, wrapped up in jeans and a filthy zip-up hoodie, with bulky muscular shoulders and eyes blazing like blue fires.

"Shit." I stumble backward, pulling Charlie with me. "What do you want?"

"You are forgetting about me," he accuses me, his voice a pleasant low rumble. "About us, Wendy."

"Uh-oh, he's cuckoo," Charlie breathes, "come, let's go—"

"Us? What are you talking about?" I dig my heels in, for some reason needing to talk to him, even though rationally I know it's the worst idea ever. "There's never been an us, we were never involved—"

He cocks his head quizzically to the side. "Us, the Lost Boys."

"The Lost Boys," I repeat, wheezing a little. "Oh, God."

"What is this about? What aren't you telling me?" Charlie turns on me, eyes narrowed. "Did you sleep with him? And some... random boys?"

"No, I..." I stop again, unsure. "I don't know."

"I tied you up in bed," he says, his voice sharpening. "Twisted your nipples. Forced my way into you. You screamed."

"What?" I say. "No."

"The Twins used their guns to fuck you. Tink almost lost control, too, but even then he couldn't let go of his past. He was getting there, though, because you were on the Island, and now they're all in pain—"

"Good Lord, this is enough," Charlie says, pulling out her phone, her face a mask of outrage and fear, "Stay away, I warn you, I got pepper spray! I'm calling the cops, you pervert psycho!"

"No." I reach for her phone, "Charlie, wait—"

He grabs the phone from her hand and dashes it to the ground. Charlie shrieks and drags me away from him, but I resist.

There's something about him, and I half-recall talking to him recently. I think I remember his name.

"Peter," I whisper.

"Yeah," he says. "That's me."

"What are you doing, Dee?" Charlie's voice is high-pitched and she's still trying to pull me away. "Come on, we have to go! He's crazy!"

"I know," I whisper.

He's watching me from under his long black lashes, head tipped back a little, as if assessing me. Or waiting for my next move. He's really handsome under all the grime, I realize with a start, with those blue eyes and angular cheekbones, a fine mouth and a square jaw, and his body is trim and muscular.

Sexy.

And what he said...

A handsome male face bowed over me, pain and pleasure as he thrusts into me, and I arch up against him, craving more.

"I never kiss."

"Wendy?" Charlie is staring at me, holding her purse in one hand and gripping my arm with the other, ready to run but curious about my blankness, no doubt. "Snap out of it. Talk to me."

"It's Peter," I whisper, "that's his name."

"Wait, you're serious?" Charlie gapes at me. "You *know* him?"

"Yeah."

"Did you really sleep with him? Is all he's saying true?"

"I'm... not sure," I whisper.

Charlie stops pulling on my arm. "Christ, girl. But—"

"Come with us," I tell Peter who blinks those ridiculously long lashes. He *is* ridiculously handsome and it's not helping with the confusion. "To our apartment."

"Wendy!" Charlie hisses. "What the hell? No way! He can't just come—"

"For dinner," I go on, trying to ignore Charlie's panic. "To talk."

"Fine," he says, as if it's a concession, a compromise. "To talk."

"Jesus, what is going on with you?" Charlie releases my arm and takes a step away from me, a frown on her face. "We don't invite random strangers into our home. That's a rule."

"You said he saved my life," I argue. "He's not a random stranger."

"I'm a specific stranger," he says and a smirk twitches at his sexy mouth.

"Yeah," I mutter. "And you need to eat."

"Do I?" he asks.

"Yeah."

He's thin, thinner than I... than I remember. How can I remember him and at the same time not? He's lost weight and black circles ring those gorgeous blue eyes.

"Can you cook?" I hear his voice in my head and frown, a headache starting behind my eyes. Did that happen? Was it a dream?

God, what's wrong with me?

———

We head back home and indeed it feels like a strange dream, having a furious and paled-lipped Charlie on one side —a few paces ahead, in fact, because she's too angry to even look at me—and the handsome junkie on the other.

I'm so aware of him as we make our way toward the apartment, crossing the street and walking on the sidewalk, that it's messing with my head.

I can actually smell him—and it's not rank sweat and trash, but male musk and sexy spice.

Which makes no sense. He lives on the street.

I'm aware of his looks, too, because the more I stare at him, the more handsome he seems. I'm caught in the sweep of those lashes, the curve of his mouth, the sharpness of his cheekbones, the dark wings of his brows.

He doesn't look much older than my twenty years, but something in his gaze and the set of his jaw feels hard and knowledgeable.

Experienced.

Scarred by the world.

Which isn't a big surprise, considering how he lives, I tell myself. Without a roof over his head. Doing God knows what for his next hit. His muscular body and a dark scar vanishing into the neckline of his filthy hoodie speak of fights, violence and pain.

He probably isn't used to dinner invitations. No wonder he looked like that at me earlier.

"You probably think I'm stupid," I whisper. "Gullible and naïve, to invite you over."

"No," he says, "I don't think that."

"I don't think you'd hurt me. Charlie says…" I glance at my friend, the rigid line of her back. "She says you saved me from a thug the other day. I apparently said so. So… did you?"

He rolls his big shoulders in a shrug. "Might have."

Charlie harrumphs. I understand why she's upset and worried, but I need to speak to this man and he commands all of my attention right now.

As we approach the building entrance, I slow down. "It's here," I say.

"I know," he replies.

"Oh."

"I'm not going in there with him," Charlie says. Obviously, his answer hasn't earned him any cookie points.

"I'm sorry," I whisper. "I need to talk to him, though. Why don't you go stay with Meredith and come back later?"

Meredith is Charlie's sister and though they don't meet that often, they are on good terms.

"But I can't leave you alone with him, either," Charlie protests, turning around to face me, rolling her eyes. "Wendy—"

"Please. I'll be fine."

"How would you know that? Wendy, no." Then she sighs dramatically. "Oh, Baby Jesus, you have that look on your face…"

"What look?"

"The look that says you have made up your mind and nothing I do or say can change it," she says. "Am I right?"

"I have to talk to him." I will her to understand, to read my face and see that this is important even if I'm not exactly sure why, but Charlie just seems to get upset all over again.

Obviously, my face is written in a different language.

"Fine, then," she hisses. "If tomorrow the cops call me because they found your corpse in the apartment, I'll… I'll…"

"You'll what?"

With a small sound of annoyance, apparently unable to think up a good punishment for a corpse, she turns on her high heel and leaves.

Peter frowns after her, then coughs—an unsettling, rattling, ugly sound.

Before I ask if he's okay, he wipes the back of his hand over his mouth and nods at me. "Talk?" he suggests.

And so, I lead the way into my apartment, not sure whether I'm the biggest idiot or just a medium-strength one.

I mean, Charlie is right. What the hell am I doing?

3

WENDY

He stands in the middle of the apartment as I close the door behind him, kick my shoes off and shrug off my jacket. It occurs to me that he isn't wearing one and that his hoodie is wet. He has to be freezing.

So I dial up the heating and walk into the kitchen to see what there is to eat. I open the fridge, study its contents. Something non-moldy would be best. I'm really not a cook but I can swing some pasta and sauce from a jar when I have to.

"Spaghetti okay?" I ask him and start when I find him right behind me. I stumble back a step. "Jesus, you scared me."

He's looking at me with an intensity in his eyes I can't read.

Lifting a hand, he pulls down the zipper of his hoodie, long fingers closing around a trinket hanging from a thin chain around his neck. Then he rubs at his chest.

I follow the movement with my gaze, staring because he's so built. His chest and shoulders are wide, though his hips are narrow and his legs long.

He's built like an athlete.

Powerful.

Sexy.

On the smooth chest over the torn tank top he's wearing under the hoodie, I see thin white marks, like scars, a match for the thin white lines on his corded forearms.

Shouldn't there be... dark designs, black ink swirling in spirals and zigzagging lines, full sleeves of ink on his arms, and—

"Spaghetti is fine," he says. "So, you can cook after all."

That's a strange comment.

"Did I ever say I couldn't?" I move away from him, mainly to stop staring and to stop seeing things that aren't there. I bang around in the cupboards, getting the pasta and the sauce, and fill the pot with water.

"Something along those lines," he says.

"When?"

"In Neverland."

I freeze, having just placed the pot on the fire, the name striking me like a blow. "Where is that?"

"You know where. You do remember things, Wendy. Try harder to—" He coughs again, presses his fist to his mouth. "Dammit."

"Are you sick? Peter..." I gasp. His hand is spattered with blood. "Oh, my God. You got TB or something?"

"No. I'm fine."

"You're not *fine*. Nobody coughing blood is fine," I whisper. "Are you... Are you dying?"

He starts. Wipes his hand on his pants. "Probably."

Jesus. It's all a déjà vu. I asked him this once and he replied the exact same thing, and—

"Wendy..." He reaches for me and I let him touch my cheek. What am I doing? "I don't need dinner or your concern. But I do need your help."

"What do you need?" I whisper.

"I need you to remember. I need you to come back."

"Remember what? Go where?" I shake my head. "No."

"Fuck." His jaw clenches. "I was hoping... but why should I ever hope? When will I finally learn my fucking lesson?"

I glance helplessly at the water-filled pot on the stove, the pack of spaghetti and the jar of Italian sauce sitting on the counter, and draw a shaky breath. "That's not fair. I really don't remember much, and what I do remember makes no sense. Stay for dinner."

"I can't stay," he says, regret shining so starkly in his voice it's hard to call him a liar.

"But it's still early."

His blue eyes look black like pits right now. "I can't stay in the human world much longer. I'm being pulled back. Can't fight it much longer."

"Peter—"

"Remember us, Wendy," he says softly. "Come back to us."

"I can't. My life is here. I barely... know you, I..."

He reaches for me but lets his hand fall before he touches me. "You changed the island. Changed me. Gave me hope."

"I just... don't believe that. I don't think there's an island, and that you came from there, that I was ever there—"

"You have to face your fears, Wendy," he goes on as if he hasn't heard me. "Face the sea. Face the water."

I suck a sharp breath. "How do you know about that?"

"Hell." He coughs again. "We depend on you, Wendy. Our lives. Our souls. The island is sinking and we're being torn apart. What you see here is a reflection of what is happening over there, and that's because you haven't faced your nightmares and haven't solved your problems."

"Now wait a minute," I breathe, heat crawling up my neck. "You don't know me and don't get to judge me like that."

He finally closes the distance between us, slides his hand around my neck to cup the back of my head, holding me very still. "Don't I?" His voice has gone low and dangerous, and for some reason, my body reacts. My nipples stiffen painfully and

I clench down below. "Damn, you react so beautifully. You smell like roses and sugar when I touch you, when you get so wet—"

"Stop it." But I don't move, breathing shallowly. "Stop."

"I haven't done anything yet. Not like I did on the island when I had you tied to the bed and took you like that, where you couldn't refuse, couldn't fight. You liked it."

"I can't have. I'd never." But my body betrays me. I'm wet between my legs. I'm burning.

He chuckles, low and dark, as if he knows exactly what's happening to me.

"It doesn't mean anything," I breathe. "This doesn't mean anything."

That he can play my body like an instrument, wringing reactions out of it I didn't know were possible with such an ungentle touch; *because* of such an ungentle touch.

That he apparently knows my body better than I do.

"You're right. It doesn't mean anything." He releases me and something like disappointment washes through me, though it can't be, right?

Then...

"Try to remember," he whispers, his eyes pleading, the quiet assurance and sexy arrogance seeping out of them, leaving them flat like mirrors. "Remember the assaults of the Reds, the songs of the mermaids, the Lost Boys, and the house in the woods. Remember the cliffs and the clearings, remember the blood and the pain and the pleasure. Remember that you don't know us but you seemed like you wanted to, like you wanted to save us."

"But..."

He grips the pendant around his neck, releases it. It's a silver thimble, I see now.

Wait, isn't that mine?

"Goodbye, Wendy. Take care." With a soft groan, he turns

around and heads for the door leaving me to stare after him, unable to move.

He was supposed to stay for dinner, stay to talk, explain why I feel this way, why I feel like I know him, that all he says is true when it's impossible.

Why I'm letting him into my home, into my head, like he belongs here.

Why I want to take care of him when he's a stranger, a—

King.

I frown. *Whatever, Dee,* I tell myself. *A king? What the hell?*

He's brainwashing you, probably going to ask for money any second now, tell you he's a long lost relative, your husband perhaps from another life, or that you have amnesia and he's been looking for you since you vanished on your honeymoon in the Bahamas, or that he's been in an accident and simply needs help.

And you're so naïve and ready to give it to him because he's handsome and obviously sick and tormented. Florence Nightingale syndrome, isn't that what they call it? Being drawn to broken men and trying to fix the unfixable?

Do I want to fix him, though? Or just... *help*? Surely a dinner is not the same thing as giving away my savings to someone.

The way he'd cradled my head, the things he'd made me feel...

Walking over to the window, I watch him exit the building and cross the street, his messy black hair glinting almost blue in the light of a lamppost. Why does he feel so familiar?

Why does he *act* so familiar? As if he knows me, not just my body and its surprising reactions, but deeper. As if he knows my mind. As if he's known me all my life.

Instead of laughing at the notion, I frown harder. Why did his words bring images to my mind? Who is he?

Under the next street lamp, he turns his head and a jolt goes through me. I throw the window open in the cold night air and lean out.

"You," I whisper as memory slams into my head like a fist—not the memory he wanted me to retrieve, though, as it's not a memory of an island or Never-whatever-land—but of the day someone dragged me out of the waves when I was little.

Saving my life.

It's not the face, exactly, that triggers the memory but the collection of features, coming together like a puzzle in the sputtering light.

The wide set of his shoulders, the contrast of his pale skin and dark hair, the shape of his face, the way he holds himself, the way he turned, glancing over his shoulder.

No way...

It can't be.

I'm seeing things. Literally *seeing things* when no such things exist. I mean, what would be the odds that my childhood savior who vanished without a word, without leaving behind an address, phone or name, is this man?

Only one way to find out.

4

TINK

"Stay down, you idiot," I hiss, grabbing Wes' arm and hauling him back down. "They'll see us."

"Fucking let go. I can't see Colt." He yanks his hand free—mostly because he catches me by surprise with his move—and runs toward the shore.

"Fuck. Fuck!" By Arawn's hairy balls, these two will be the death of me.

If the mermaids or the Red don't get me first, that is, and that's without counting Hook and his friends.

"Wes!" I hurry after him, boots skidding down the slope leading to the craggy beach below, trying to make the Twins out. "Wes, wait, damn you!"

One happy family, this island.

And Peter has been away too long. I can't keep dragging his shadow around. It's trying to attach itself to me, like a parasite, a leech, all anger and violence and snarling, and I got enough of that shit of my own, thank you very fucking much.

I don't need Peter's, too.

In his case, all that violence isn't really his, or at least it's not always a part of him, not since his shadow detached and changed, since he'd had to stitch it back on, to find his way back to it.

I don't need a shadow. I don't want a soul.

The world is bad enough without one.

Finally, I see the pair of idiots on a rock. Colt seems stuck and Wes is trying to free his foot from a crack. Below, the sea shimmers with the backs and tails of mermaids.

They're gathering.

"Wes!" I slide down the slope and jump over a crack, and then another, heading for them. "Hurry up, you dimwits, they're coming!"

I reach them as the first mermaid starts crawling up the rock, dragging herself up with her claws, her sharp teeth clacking together.

Wes is still trying to free Colt's foot and I drop to my knees beside him, grabbing and pulling on his ankle. "What the fuck did you do? What were you doing down here?"

Colt only grinds his teeth and works his jaw as he fights to free himself from the crack.

"Asshole." I yank harder on his leg. "Answer me."

"You're not the king," Colt snarls, all bad attitude and anger. "I don't answer to you."

Before I can tell him exactly what I think of his comment, his foot comes free and we all fall back on our asses, cursing.

"Whoa. Mermaids!" Colt scrambles to his feet, only to fall back down with a groan. "Fuck."

I hope his foot isn't broken. Asshole is too heavy to carry.

With a shake of my head and a huff, I slide an arm around him and get him up. "Come on, assholes, let's move it."

Wes jumps to his feet and pulls out his gun as the scraping sound of the mermaids climbing the rock grows louder. "Go, I'll cover you."

"You'd better not stay behind and get eaten, hear me?" I

growl and he gives me a surprised look. "What? I don't look forward to being the last sane man standing on the island."

"Define sane."

"Shut your mouth," I mutter.

Yeah, that's all. I just hate the thought of staying here on my own. I'd get bored to death prior to getting eaten, and that would just suck.

Right?

It's not that I give a shit about these guys, or that Peter's absence is already a hole in my chest, or that Wendy's departure tore something inside of me. I don't even know what the hell it was.

All I know is that it's bleeding darkness and pain into my veins.

"Watch where you're going, Tinkers," Colt calls out as we almost slide back down the slope we're trying to climb. "Can you see Wes?"

I crane my neck to look. "He's following us."

Colt lets out a breath. He was worried, just like Wes was worried about him.

How does that feel, huh, having someone so concerned over your wellbeing? Like, really concerned, not just pretending. Going down dangerous slopes to help them, save them.

I try not to think that I just did that, too, and what it means.

It means nothing.

"Seriously, man, what were you doing down there?" I mutter.

"I thought I saw something, all right?"

"Saw what?"

"I thought I saw Peter," he says, his dark gaze shuttering, turning his eyes into black mirrors.

"Great, now we're seeing things," I grumble. "It was about time."

"What? You expected it?"

"I expect everything thrown at us now that Wendy left," I say. "She's the first Wendy to go back. The island isn't happy not to have tasted her flesh and the rest of them are pleased for this chance to take us apart. So yeah, I expected all sorts of things, so keep your eyes peeled and your head on straight."

"Or else, what, we die?" He snorts. "I've lived way too long already."

I try to ignore the stab in my chest his words produce. "This isn't about you, or about us. We keep fighting."

"If it's never about us," he says softly, "then we don't have any hope, and without hope, what's left?"

"Nothing," I tell him, making my voice hard. "It's all hopeless. Get over it. We don't get the luxury of stopping because of despair."

Hopeless. It's how my life has been since I can remember. But the truth is... when Wendy arrived, that changed. I don't even fucking know why.

It was a trick, a trap.

Good things always are.

"I'm fucking starving," Wes says, leaning against a trunk, twirling his gun on his forefinger. He has a gash down one arm where a dead branch caught him. I'm more concerned about Colt's ankle but Colt is stubbornly silent, sitting on a rock. "I could eat anything right now. Even tree bark is starting to seem appealing."

He says it lightly, like a joke. Problem is, we haven't had any food in days.

"Have you ever tried bark?" I ask. "Some are nasty."

He laughs like I'm telling a joke, but I've had bark and it made me sick like a dog. I was curious about whether he grew up similarly to me, but that was unlikely in the first place. I'm the one who grew up in Faerie. The one kicked out to live in the human world, alone in the woods. The one raised by monks. The mongrel Fae.

The one who is different.

"These are oaks," I say after a while, glancing down. "We can eat the acorns."

"Acorns? I'm not a pig."

"No," I say, bending and picking an acorn from the ground, "you're a fucking idiot. These are edible acorns."

"Look at this domestic side of you," Colt says. "So you do cook after all?"

"I'm not cooking them," I clarify. "I just eat them."

Wes bites into one. Spits it out. "It's fucking bitter."

"Fucking idiot, like I said. Haven't you ever watched a squirrel eat? Only eat the top of the acorn, discard the bitter part near the cap."

"No, I've never watched squirrels eat." Wes throws the acorn away with a flick of his fingers. "What the fuck, Tink. Not all of us grew up in nature, hugging trees."

"Fuck you," I breathe.

"Hugging trees is so out of style," Colt mutters. "Wes, stop being an ass."

Wes picks up another acorn and gives me a calculating look, as if he thinks I'm lying. "And how do you know that the discarded part is bitter?"

"When you're left to fend for yourself in nature," I snarl, "you try everything, hoping it's edible. You make mistakes. You learn."

Huge, puking-your-guts-out, hoping-to-die mistakes. A good thing even half a Fae is hard to kill.

Half a Fae means half dead anyway. What are the Fae but ghosts?

"Aren't you the son of a Faerie king? What the hell happened?" Colt smirks. "Did they decide you were such a nuisance they threw you in the pigsty to eat acorns?"

"Eat with the pigs," Wes chuckles.

"That would have been good," I mutter. "The pigs were given food every day. I wasn't. I was expected to die like the good royal bastard I am."

Wes's gaze darkens. "Hey, hey, Tink. Fuck, I wasn't thinking. It was a joke."

"Yeah, it was a real hoot," I say.

"Jesus, Tink," Colt says, getting up, "sorry, man, I just—"

"And you know what? Enough talk." I throw an acorn at him. "Eat up and let's move."

"Stop giving us orders," Colt snarls. "You're not Peter."

I grab his shirt and haul him until we're nose to nose. "I'm keeping his throne warm for him. Didn't he tell you?"

On cue, Peter's shadow unfurls behind me, over me, growling like a beast.

Colt jerks away from me. "Holy fuck."

"Is that...?" Wes licks his lips, eyes wide. "Is that Peter's Shadow?"

"That's right." My voice is a growl, too. "What's the matter, forgot that's what always happens when he goes away?"

"I haven't been here all that long," Wes argues. "Only met one other Wendy before this one came along."

I look away, clench my fists. Call the shadow back into me. It's like trying to hug a rabid dog. "I keep forgetting you're still a goddamn baby."

He makes a choking, disbelieving noise in his throat. "Fuck you so much, Tink."

"No, thanks."

Time is a strange, relative thing here. Colt and Wes are apparently of the same age, yet Colt has been here for more than a century. Wes only a few decades.

In comparison, I feel positively ancient—and again it

doesn't have to do so much with time itself as with the experiences it contains.

With Peter's shadow more or less contained, twitching as it scratches at the inside of my body, I bend to gather more acorns.

To my surprise, Wes does the same. "Ever wonder why Peter has an acorn hanging around his neck?" he mutters.

"He doesn't anymore," I inform them. "He gave it to Wendy."

Colt whistles. "That's a big commitment. He's had that acorn for centuries. It's almost as if she is the one, isn't it? Though, of course, she... kind of left."

"But why would he have an acorn?" Wes insists, picking up one and biting into it. He makes a face. "Man, they are still bitter."

"Look for the golden ones," I say. "And peel the skin. It's bitter, too."

"Couldn't you have said?"

"The corns of the golden oaks of Faerie produce acorns that taste sweet with a faint bitter aftertaste. Look." I peel one. "The inside is light, a pale yellow. If it's black or blue don't eat it."

"Peter's acorn is golden, too," Wes says, peeling his acorn.

"Peter has an acorn because it is his sigil of power," I bite out.

"Sigil?"

"He's the thunder god."

Wes laughs. "Peter isn't a *god,* asshole, though he often thinks he is."

"As if you'd know how gods are made." I scowl down at my hands, hating how his absence aches, how the fear that he's not coming back eats at me. "I've had a fucking vision, saw him in all his glory."

"Shut the front door," Wes mutters.

"But you're right," I say. "He's stuck in this twilight zone, this dispute between worlds, like the rest of us. Currently stuck in the human world, in fact, and who knows when he's coming back—"

A cold, hard something grips my leg and wrenches me away. My back slams into the ground, knocking out my breath, and black patches spread in my vision as I'm dragged away—by the leg, and what the fuck—?

"Tink!" Colt yells. "Fuckers!"

Fuckers?

Oh, fucking shit...

Reds.

The monster is dragging me through the sparse woods toward the ruins of the city and I'm still too dazed to move.

How did it get so close? How didn't it make a noise? You'd think the metal parts would make some racket, I think dizzily as my arm smashes into a trunk, as my other leg hits a rock.

Ow, fuck. Fuck! Think, I tell myself desperately, *think!*

Trying to slow the going, I grab at bushes and trunks and low-sprouting branches as the Red inexorably makes its way through the thicket.

At least the monster is alone, can't see any other of its kind around. Is it a loner? Normally they attack as a pack.

I have to stop him so I can somehow get free. Its claw around my ankle is like a vise. Muscles tensing, wrenching in my shoulder, I grab at a low branch and hang on, wishing... wishing that Peter was here.

He's... he's the only one I trust. The Twins remind me too much... of other things. I *need* Peter to return.

Like a damsel in distress, waiting for her knight.

You can't fucking depend on anyone, I remind myself. *What the fuck? You only ever have yourself, so fight!*

With a savage snarl, I grab at another branch and wrench my body back, slowing the Red once more, fumbling at my hip for my sword.

Goddammit. Why can't I get to it? My fingers are stiff, my blood like ice in my veins.

Then behind me, I hear Colt and Wes calling out my name, crashing through the undergrowth.

It takes me a moment to accept it's real, that they're coming after me.

Why is it so hard to think they care for me?

The Red stops, turns its huge head and roars, saliva dripping from a mouth like a shark's. It yanks on my ankle and I curse, losing my grip on the branch and the hilt of my sword, too slow to pull it out of its sheath as the Red starts moving again.

Changing direction.

Dragging me toward the shore.

"No. Fuck, no." I struggle, grabbing at anything I can find, my palms stinging and bleeding.

"Tink!" The Twins are still coming after me and the Red is now descending a gentle slope toward the heaving sea, and through slitted eyes, I make out forms.

Mermaids.

"No." I struggle harder, drag my nails on the ground to stop. "No!"

"Well done," the mermaid says in her grating voice, reaching out a clawed hand toward me. "Give him to us."

Then the Twins are there.

Almost too late.

"Tink, you okay?" Wes is almost beside me, now, skidding down the slope. "What the hell."

My heart is thrashing inside my chest.

"What the fuck," Colt snarls, coming up on my other side, drawing a knife from somewhere, "are the Reds working together with the mermaids now?"

He slashes at the Red's hand and suddenly I'm free and rolling down to the rocky beach.

Fucking double *ow*.

I'm free—but the mermaids reach for me. I roll out of reach, their claws inches from my skin.

Then a bang rings out, rattling my bones as I roll to a stop and try to catch my breath.

Colt's gun smokes.

The other mermaids slow their advance.

"It begins," the mermaid at the front says. "It's almost upon us. The Night of Nights."

"What the fuck is she talking about?" Wes snaps.

I drag myself up the rocks, my ankle throbbing, my palms shredded as Colt slides down the slope toward me, his gun raised—

And then *he* steps out of thin air and stumbles to his knees. "Fuck," he hisses. "Tink."

"Peter!"

He's here. As if he's heard my earlier thoughts, he appears out of nowhere, and now he's kneeling on the rocks, coughing, head bowed. He's obviously just returned from the human world, the gray hoodie he's wearing spattered with blood, his face white as a sheet.

Sucky timing, like always, that guy, at least for him. Good timing for me, though, when he saved my ass that long ago.

Time to return the favor.

"Peter," I yell, *move!*" One of the mermaids is crawling up the beach, clawed hands reaching for him, and I stagger toward him. "Peter, goddammit!"

The mermaid makes a grab for him. I shove him back, getting between her and her prey—and the mermaid sinks her poisonous fangs into my leg.

Shit.

This day has gone straight to hell.

5

PETER

I've barely landed in Neverland, winded from the pummeling forces trying to tear me apart as I crossed between the worlds, and the goddamned foul-mouthed half-Fae slams into me without warning and throws me on my back on the rocks.

God *fuck*.

At least I am in the right place, and I can hear the Twins. They're yelling Tink's name and cursing.

"Well, sorry I interrupted your little argument," I mutter, then groan when my shadow grabs me, sinking its talons into my scar.

Attaching itself to me once more.

"Hello to you, too," I grind out and slowly sit up, swallowing another groan as my shadow sinks its hooks into me deeper, anchoring itself on bone and sinew. "Miss me?"

"Peter!" Wes comes barreling toward me, grabs my arm and pulls, almost wrenching it out of its socket. "We gotta go."

"Yeah, okay, gimme a sec. What's the fucking rush?" I grumble as he hauls me to my feet, not giving me a goddamn second to catch my breath. "Relax."

"Mermaids," he says succinctly and I tense.

"Fuck," I breathe.

"Yeah. Peter, come on." Wes is pulling on my arm, and this time I let him pull, let him get me moving. "We need to get away from the water."

"Pan against the Mermaid Queen," I mutter.

"What?"

"That's what Tink always says. Pan against the Mermaid Queen. Where is he? He shoved me just now."

"Colt is helping him."

That makes me stop cold in my tracks and glance around, trying to locate him. "*Helping* him? Why, what's wrong?"

"Nothing, just... A Red came out of nowhere and grabbed him, dragged him over here. We caught up with him before the mermaids got him but his ankle is probably sprained."

Okay, that doesn't sound too bad, though running is crucial, with the Reds and mermaids after our asses...

"How have things been?" Colt helps me over the crest of the steep slope and we're on level ground again.

My lungs still feel crushed, and I wonder if I'll ever breathe right again, and my shadow snaps at my back, pulling on the scar, pulling on every raw nerve ending.

"Peachy," Wes growls, which isn't entirely like him, more like Colt. Not a good sign at all.

"Spill."

"Keep walking," he says, "so *we* don't fucking spill down, and then we can talk."

"Wes!" Colt's voice carries over the rising wind off the sea that brings the smell of salt and dead things. "Over here."

"I'm okay." I step away from Wes, shaking the damn dizziness and breathlessness off me. "Let's go."

"Did you find Wendy?" Wes asks as we jog toward Colt and Tink. "I gather she didn't wanna come back with you."

"We talked," I rumble. "I did my best to convince her. I think she's considering it."

"Yeah, right."

He doesn't believe it. Not sure I believe it myself. But we have other more pressing issues to consider right now—and I'm talking apart from the island crumpling with only a lone rock left standing in the heaving sea, crowned with a few trees and the ruined city at its center, the rest of its area taken up by monsters and a rival gang.

If you can call Hook's army a gang.

Still. More pressing matters.

Like Tink.

He's fighting with Colt who is apparently still trying to pull him away from the brink of the slope leading down to the deadly sea, but Tink is having none of it.

"Don't fucking touch me!" he yells, trying to punch Colt. He punches right and left, kicking and twisting, while Colt does his best to hold on to him and avoid getting hit.

Which is... weird. It makes me frown. Tink isn't clumsy. His aim is never off.

"Dammit, sit still. It's just me," Colt says.

"So what?" Tink pants. "Stay away."

"Man, you got issues. I'm not the one who hurt you."

"Let go of me, asshole." Tink staggers a few steps away, his face pale, the pink in his copper hair gone black. The dark strands stick to his cheeks, his jaw, his neck. "What the fuck are you doing?"

"What's this about? Did you hit your head, too?" Colt lifts his hands. "I'm trying to help you, Tinker. You're injured."

"I said I'm fine."

"What the fuck," I mutter, slowing down as I approach, grabbing Wes' arm to stop him from rushing in. "Something's wrong."

"Damn right something's wrong." Wes yanks his arm free. "Tink is being an ass again."

"No, that's... Wait, Wes. Stay back."

He sighs. "Why? Think he'll listen to you?"

It's possible. You never know with the goddamn Tinker, that unpredictable Fae side of him, but maybe.

"Tink!" I yell, walking toward him. "Stand down, Tink!"

He turns toward me like a cornered animal—and my shadow stretches, reaching for him. It touches him and he hisses, jerking.

"Gather your shadow back, *King*," he spits out, eyes wild. "I've had enough trouble fighting it in your absence."

I chuckle. "My shadow *molested* you while I was away?"

"Fuck you," he growls. "Nobody *molested* me, you... You just..." A look of surprise crosses his face, then he folds down on his knees and drops forward, slamming his hands down, into the soft soil. "What the hell..."

"Tink!" I'm already running. At least he doesn't resist when I grab his shoulders, looking him over for injuries. I don't see anything. No blood gushing. No torn flesh. "What's the matter?"

"I'm just... fine," he slurs.

Fuck. I haul him up and then sling him over my shoulder. "We should go. This place isn't safe. We should go home."

"No place is safe," Wes says. "And there's no home left to go to."

"The house is *gone*?" I still have Tink slung over my shoulder. He's stirring but not struggling, which scares the hell out of me, but my main goal is to get them all someplace safe. "What happened?"

"The island is vanishing. Parts of it just... poof. Disappear."

I step over a rock, tighten my grip on Tink's legs. "They crumble into the sea?"

"That only happens at the edges," Wes says. "At the center, it just... compresses, I guess, swallowing up parts."

"It's because she doesn't want to face her past," I whisper. "She pushes the memories down deep. So they fade instead of becoming clearer."

"Fucking great," Colt says. "Just... great."

"That means she is the one, right?" Wes mutters.

"I'm starting to think that she's the one if she decides to be the one," I tell them.

"That's... new." Colt stares at me.

"Take advantage of my memory while it still works," I mutter, clinging to clarity for as long as it will last. My mind is only clear when I'm in the human world. The moment I return here, it starts to fray.

First things first.

If we have no home to go to, then the small clearing will have to do for now. I lower Tink to the ground and he grunts, rolling on his side.

"Peter," he breathes, dark lashes lifting. His green eyes are dazed.

"I'm right here." I crouch down beside him. "What happened?"

"I told you," Wes says from behind me, "the Red—"

"Not that. I told you, something's wrong." I pat Tink down, checking him for injuries again, and that's when I see them, the red marks on his calf. "Fuck, Tink..."

"Holy shit. A mermaid got him," Colt says, his voice unexpectedly hushed.

"How did you...?" Then I remember Tink shoving me away, down on the beach. "You took my place," I whisper. "Pushed me away and the mermaid got you. Took the poison for me."

"Stop it," Tink says. His eyes are clearing.

"But—"

"Don't make a big deal out of it. I didn't do it for you."

"No?"

"No, I did it for me," Tink says.

My throat closes at all the possibilities that answer contains. "You fucker."

"I'll be fine," Tink says, slowly sitting up. "Make camp and stop hovering. I'm half-Fae. The poison doesn't affect the Fae."

"You're also half-human," I growl.

"Nobody's perfect."

"Tink—"

"Better me than you," he says.

"That's bullshit. Don't you ever fucking say things like that." My shadow curls around me, whispering dark things in my ear, reaching again for Tink.

"Keep that thing the fuck away from me," Tink snarls.

Goddammit. The last thing he needs is violence from me, from any of us. I pull back. "What did my shadow do when I wasn't here? What did it do to you?"

"Nothing." He grabs a rock, throws it to thunk against a tree trunk. A shudder goes through him. My shadow has touched him. He snarls, showing his sharp canines. "Fuck off!"

"Tinker." Colt crouches down on his other side. "You have to calm down or else the poison will act faster."

"Why is he so bad off?" I whisper.

"I think I know," Wes says, coming to stand beside me as I straighten. "We weather the poison from their claws just fine, but their teeth... We managed never to get bitten before. The sea was further, we had dry land between us and them."

"He can't..." I grind my jaw. "Wes..."

"I know."

"He saved me once," Tink is telling Colt. He's grabbed Colt's hand and is squeezing the shit out of Colt's fingers. His eyes are dark and yet too bright. The poison is already acting. "That's what he does: saves you and then possesses you, makes you need him, makes you want him. Crave him. Maybe love him even."

Oh, hell. "Tink..."

"You don't?" Tink insists, staring hard at Colt. "You don't feel that way?"

"You're not yourself," Colt says. He lifts his head, meets my gaze. His is pleading with me to do something.

Maybe to understand what Tink is saying.

Tink is talking about me, and the knot in my chest is growing bigger, tighter. He's saying things I'd hoped to hear over the centuries but never spoke them myself. Things that have fucked up my head.

But then Tink hauls Colt toward him, a sudden movement, pulling Colt off balance, and Tink draws his other hand back and punches him in the face. "I said don't touch me," he snarls.

And lets Colt fall back on his ass, a stunned look on his face.

Dammit.

Tink has lost it.

Wes rushes to pull a growling Colt away before he attacks Tink, while I reach for a snarling, struggling Tink, and while this is more like him, like the Tink who first came to me all that long ago, a wild animal, it's also a testament to our change.

Our change wrought through this island.

Our relationship, our taming of each other.

Our friendship that could be so much more.

"Tink, stand down!" I yell.

He only struggles harder, his eyes turning black, his nails turning into claws, and I haul him against my body knowing full well it triggers him worse but unable to help myself.

I keep losing control.

All of us are.

We're all getting twisted out of shape, out of ourselves, unfolding in a dark dimension.

That's what mermaid poison does to you.

That's what this place does to you.

What despair does.

If Wendy doesn't come back, we won't even need the Reds, the mermaids or Hook's band to end us. One by one, we are all going to drown in our own misery and fall.

6

WENDY

"You're out of your mind," Charlie says the following morning, having returned annoyed and pissy from her sister's place. "There is no frigging way."

"Charlie, I'm telling you. He's the one who saved me from the sea as a child."

"I heard you. And I repeat, you're out of your mind." She paces our living room, hands on her hips, brows drawn low. "How is that possible, that he was the one who saved you from a mugger a few days ago, and now coincidentally he's also the guy who saved you when you were little? Are you sure your mind isn't making up things?"

"Why would my mind make up things?"

"I dunno," she says. "Because you like him? Because he's handsome?"

I grin a little. "You noticed, too?"

She sighs. "Hard not to. But Dee, he's not your savior. He can't be. Unless... did he stalk you? Is he a creepy stalker?"

"Stop that," I tell her. "It's not like that. Why do you have to be so suspicious?"

"Because you are so naïve sometimes?"

"Gee, thanks, girlfriend." I shake my head, "No, it wouldn't make any sense. He never contacted me before today. If he had wanted something, wouldn't he have made a move sooner?"

But doubt rears its ugly head, despite my protests.

"Psychopaths don't think like us, girlie." Charlie sits down beside me on the sofa and pats my hand. Her gaze is sympathetic and makes me feel a hundred times worse. Makes me feel like I've been stupid to insist, stupid to have invited him in, not to have suspected him of any wrongdoing. "Tell me what happened here. He just walked away? Are you sure he didn't steal anything?"

"No, he didn't. Yes, I'm sure. And... it's more than that," I admit. "It's more complicated."

"Meaning?"

I struggle with the words, with the recollections. "I remember... stuff. I remember him. And some other guys."

She pales. "Dee. Did he ever give you drugs? It sounds like hallucinations. Did he—?"

"I—no! Of course not." I look at her, aghast. "I hadn't even talked to him before today. Or actually..."

"Actually?"

"God, that's what I'm trying to tell you. I'm not sure." I massage my brow. A headache is blooming behind my eyes, hammering inside my skull. "I have talked to him before. Of course I have."

"And he planted ideas in your head."

"It's not like that."

Isn't it, though? God, why am I doubting myself now? He wanted me to remember and I did—I got images and saw his face, but isn't that what projection does? I remember watching a psychological thriller with a similar plot. Did he plant those ideas inside my head?

"I'll make you some hot milk," Charlie decides, getting up, "and then we'll go to bed and forget all about this guy. And you won't talk to him ever again. In fact, if I see him nearby, I'm calling the cops."

"No, Charlie." I get up, too, take her hand. "Please, don't."

Her gaze grows uncertain. "But…"

"Let me show you something."

———

"IF YOU THINK ANYTHING YOU SHOW ME WILL CONVINCE ME TO LET that psycho around you again…" Charlie grumbles as she follows me into my room.

"Please." I sit cross-legged on my bed, grab my laptop and turn it toward her. "The news article from my rescue, all those years ago. Look at the photo."

She squints down at the screen. "What about it?"

"*Look*, Charlie, just do me this favor. Look at the man."

A sigh. "Okay, I'll bite. Who is he?"

"He's the guy I told you about. From when I was little." I wave a vague hand in the air. "The one who pulled me out of the sea."

"You have a photo of him from back then?"

"A journalist snapped the picture as the police arrived. Then the man vanished."

"He *vanished*," Charlie says, disbelief shining in her voice. "You mean he ran away. Running away is never a good sign, girl. Why would a man run away if he had a clear conscience"

"Many reasons. Maybe he doesn't like cops. Who does? I'm telling you, Charlie, he's the one who saved me."

She sits down beside me on the bed. "Why were you in the sea in winter anyway?"

I press my lips together. "That's a story I don't like talking about."

Charlie leans closer, gazing at the screen. Clucks her tongue. "Okay, fine, the homeless junkie does look like the guy who saved you from the sea when you were little. I didn't even know about that, that a random stranger had pulled you out. I thought it had been your own family."

"No. Not my family," I whisper, turning the laptop back around, to stare at the picture. "And for a long time, I wasn't sure it was true. I wasn't sure that I had fallen into the sea, that I hadn't imagined it."

"*Imagined* it. But Dee..." Charlie gives me a faintly horrified look. "You *know* what happened. You are the one who told me about it."

"You're right, but... the actual memory is kinda fuzzy," I admit.

"But it was in the papers." She points at my laptop. "On the news. Well, how it all ended, at least."

I nod. "Yeah, how it ended."

"You told me that you fell in the sea from a boat, that you had been with friends, that—"

"I don't think that's how it happened," I whisper.

"Then how?"

I shake my head.

Why can't I remember?

"Who pushed you, Dee?" Charlie asks softly, and I tumble headfirst into dark water, deep and cold, murky and rife with danger. Hands reach for me, long talons tipped with black, snarling mouths open, about to sink fangs into my flesh...

"Dee?"

"I don't know," I say, my voice shaking.

"You remember that, though? Someone pushing you? You said you had gone out boating with friends."

I shrug. "Honestly, I don't know anymore. I still don't know what happened."

"Don't tell me it's repressed memories?"

"I don't have any repressed memories," I scoff.

"Sure you don't." The look she's giving me says she's calling my bluff. "So you almost drown, a stranger saves your life, and then you leave home for a year and stay with your aunt? Why?"

"Did I do that?"

"Mary and Baby Jesus, what's going on with you?" Charlie is starting to look pissed. She points at the screen of the laptop. "It says so right here, in the article. You left your family and went to live with your aunt." She pauses. "Your parents never gave a statement. Your brothers remained with your parents..."

"Yeah. Mom had a fit." I swallow hard. "When I left."

"Your mom is still at home? I always thought she had left, or passed away."

"No, she... she's fine." A black hole opens in my chest at the mention of her. I try to breathe through it.

"That's too much like fiction," Charlie whispers.

"Don't I know it."

"And you didn't remember it was him? This Peter, saving you?"

"No, I didn't. Until I saw him again."

"Okay, fine." She gnaws on her lower lip. "Let's assume it really was him and not some lookalike. That he is the guy who saved you back then, and happens now to sleep across the street. Shit like that happens. The laws of probability are infinite."

"If you say so," I tell her dubiously.

"But that doesn't mean anything. Right? It's just physics. Probability. It doesn't have to mean anything, Dee. Do you hear me? He could still be a crazy psycho killer. Stay away from him."

And although that's what I told myself earlier, what I keep telling myself, there's no way I can convince myself it's all a coincidence, or that I don't care. I need to dig deeper, find out what is going on here.

I have to talk to Peter again.

BUT PETER ISN'T ACROSS THE STREET ANYMORE. THERE'S NO SIGN of him, no sign he ever slept across from my apartment. No cardboard box, no blanket, no sleeping bag, not even any plastic wrappers and bottles.

Am I losing my mind?

I ask a few storekeepers on the same street but they say they haven't seen him lately. Maybe he now sleeps elsewhere? Maybe he left town? You never know with these lazy bums, junkies and druggies, do you?

I think of him, standing so serious and contained inside my apartment, asking me to remember. Asking for my help, but...

I stop, bracing a hand against a building façade for support as images flash behind my eyes. Two guys... Twins. I see them in my mind's eye, clear as day. Then a slender man with pink streaks in his hair, grinning. Peter, passed out on a beach as mermaids crawl up toward us, mouths full of fangs and clawed hands—

"You all right, dear?" An old lady all in pink is looking at me with concern. Rhinestones blink on her walking stick. "You look pale."

There's a sound in my ears, like the soughing of waves on a beach.

It could just be the blood rushing in my ears.

"Thank you," I whisper, "I'm okay. There's something I need to do."

"We all have our tasks and goals," she says, the words barely registering. "You should do what matters the most to you."

"You're right," I whisper. "This is what I must do."

Find Peter.

But how?

He told me how. Which is crazy. This isn't a fairytale, and I don't believe in magic, but... I think of my brothers, the money

I'm saving to get them out of the house, to come stay with me, because... because it's better if they leave.

I think of Charlie, waiting for me at the apartment, upset and worried if I'm late.

And I think of Peter. Of how insane all this is. Of the earnest look in his blue eyes, the pressure in my chest when I think he's in trouble.

I remember him saying, *"We depend on you, Wendy. Our lives. Our souls. The island is sinking and we're being torn apart."*

Yeah, this is one hundred percent crazy. If I do it, I'll be certifiable, fully insane, with bells on.

But what do I have to lose by calling out Peter's name?

Worst case scenario, I'll get some pointed fingers and laughter, some weird looks from the passersby.

Believe, I tell myself. *Believe in fairies. Believe in possibilities.*

Gripping the golden acorn hanging around my neck, I close my eyes and breathe in.

Then I yell into the early morning his name three times, as he instructed me to do.

"Peter!" I shout. "Peter! PETER!"

I believe you. I believe in you. Take me.

And the world goes black.

7

WENDY

I wake up in darkness.

For a long moment, I think I'm in my room, in my bed —only then I notice rocks digging into my back and a familiar sound.

A terrible sound.

Waves crashing against rocks, that endless back and forth of the tides that seems to match the beat of my heart.

The island.

I sit up carefully, wincing as a throb goes through my head. Did I hit it? I reach up, feel my skull but don't encounter any tender lump. Did I—?

Then the memories rush in like a flood, making me gasp and bow over my legs, pressing my hands to my face.

Waking up at the beach with Peter, the house in the woods.

Tink and the Twins, the rough sex, the weird banter.

Running from Hook's gang, running from the mermaids, from the Reds.

Peter cutting bloody lines on his arm.

Colt and Wes confessing they don't know who is the human one between them.

Tink snarling, all teeth—

"Who's there?" a male voice says, smashing the images to dust.

Oh God, oh God. I don't know this voice.

My breathing too harsh in my ears, I sit there on the ground, quiet as a mouse, curling over and making myself small. Bushes and weeds grow around me, but I don't know how well they hide me, if at all.

Heavy steps crash in the underbrush, approaching me, and I shrink more. The island is a dangerous place, I remember now, as much because of the monsters as the humans. Or human-like beings.

I hunker down, breath caught in my throat—because I came to help Peter, Tink and the Twins, and in spite of the returning memories, that's my goal. I'm sticking to it and I can't let myself get caught.

I came back in spite of them... but also thanks to them because I remember how they touched me, handled me, pleasured me, and I want to resent them for it but I can't. Not when I wanted it so much. Not when it turned out to be exactly what I needed.

My face heats as more memories come back, slamming into me just like their cocks had, making me breathless and wet with arousal.

"There's nobody there, Captain Hook!" the man calls out, his steps moving away.

Hook!

"Keep looking," Hook—Jas—says, his proximity startling me. "I'm sure I heard something. And what's this smell of roses? We don't have any roses on the island."

"Call me Jas," he'd told me.

"Let's get you home," he'd said, and he'd kept his word.

"It's not Peter and the Lost Boys, that much is for sure," the man says. "Our scouts said there was smoke rising from the east coast. That's where they are now, and we—"

"They move about," Jas says. "Now their home is gone, they make camp wherever they can. But they're cunning. They could be lighting a fire on the east coast and then sneaking up on us here."

"We'll cut them down where they stand, Captain," the man says dutifully.

"You idiot," Jas says so low I can barely hear him and he's standing almost on top of me. "That was never what I wanted."

I freeze, my hand automatically curling around the pendant hanging from my neck—Peter's acorn. What does Jas mean? Isn't he the sworn enemy of the Lost Boys? What's going on here?

And then another memory unfurls, slowly like a flower, of the boys talking about how Hook had saved them from the Reds.

It's a fuzzy memory, intertwined with other... more interesting images and sensations, so it's not very clear, but they said he had intervened, saving their lives.

My head is pounding by now, the hail of memories taking the headache up a few notches, each memory hitting like a jagged stone.

What is going on here?

Eventually Jas wanders away, and I let out a controlled breath. Okay, it's okay. They didn't find me. I need to get myself together and go find the Lost Boys.

They'll know what is happening, what is supposed to happen. Peter asked for my help, and though I still don't know how I could aid him, I'm here now for whatever he needs.

I shiver when that word—*need*—brings a new onslaught of memories.

Holy shit, did the Twins really pleasure me with their *guns*? And I'm going back to that?

You loved it, a little voice says in my head as I slowly unfold and stand up. *Every second of it. Admit it. You frigging loved everything they did to you.*

No, no...

Is this why you came back? The sex and the violence, running away from your boring life to the excitement of danger?

Is it?

Just go. Find them.

Still clasping the golden acorn pendant in my hand, I walk in the opposite direction Hook and his men took, dazed at actually being back here, that the strange children's ritual Peter mentioned worked, wishing I knew which is the eastern coast of the island.

In the dark, all directions look the same, the island turning into a dark mass of trees and rocks, all around encompassing everything... the sea.

Shivers rack me. It's so dark. I wish morning would come already.

A sudden fear grips me that I'll stumble and fall down, to the beach, into the waves, that the black water will swallow me and that this time I'll drown and become fodder for the mermaids and the fish.

But as I move cautiously among the trees and shrubs, my heart pounding against my ribs and cold sweat running down my back, the sky lightens at the horizon, painting the sea in red and gold.

Dawn is breaking.

I stop in my tracks, staring. No way. It's as if I willed it to happen, caused the sun to rise just then.

Utterly ridiculous.

Impossible.

Improbable.

"These are your nightmares," Peter has said. *"The island is changing. Face your fears."*

No. Coincidences do happen in the world. I was never one of those people who believed in the undercurrents of fate, in changing outcomes through belief, in destiny and auras and the power of the mind. Such things had never helped or saved me before.

Why should they start now?

Maybe because you're on some sort of enchanted horror island, I think. *Because you're caught inside a nightmare and yet you're so frigging excited to see the boys again, it's not even funny. The boys that tied you up and used you.*

And made you come like nobody ever has before...

I'm crashing through the underbrush, caught in my thoughts, the lightening sky illuminating a leaf here, a branch there, the soundtrack of the hated waves still washing over me, when something feels wrong.

Well, *more* wrong, since I suddenly have a gun kissing my neck, a cold mouth pressing into my skin. I gasp, stopping so abruptly I almost fall over my feet.

Clenching my fists at my sides, I wait, my heart thumping so hard it's threatening to burst out of my chest, for something to happen.

The gun shifts a little.

A booted foot crunches on dead leaves.

"Don't move," a voice says, a familiar voice—and then, on a grunt, "What the fuck, it can't be... *Wendy?*"

———

THE HARD GRIP ON MY ARM FEELS FAMILIAR, TOO, AND strangely comforting, though it's not Peter dragging me behind him.

It's Colt.

I stare sideways at him as he marches me down a faint trail among the scraggly trees, at his clean profile, the Roman nose and firm lips, the hard cut of his jaw, the wings of his brows, the loose dark hair escaping his ponytail.

Truth is, I'm both relieved and stunned that it is him, that it's any one of them. I can't believe I found them, after all. I guess for a while there I really thought I was going crazy, that I had made them up.

Is this all in my head? It feels real. The painful press of his blunt fingertips into my flesh, the way he wrenches me forward to walk faster, keep up with him.

"Colt," I breathe.

"Hm?" He glances at me, slows down, his grip relaxing a little. "You okay?"

I grapple with what to say. Is that concern in his dark eyes? "Are you real?"

He chuckles. "Sure am. Come on, we're not far."

"From the house?"

"The house is gone," he says. "We have a camp now."

Hook had said as much, but... "Why is the house gone?"

A slight shrug of broad shoulders. "The island is falling into the sea. Parts just vanish. Any idea why?"

"You're asking *me*?"

"You're the Wendy," he mutters, frowning. "I don't fucking get it. Either you're the one or you're not. Why is this so messed up?"

"You tell me," I whisper and have to jog to keep up as his fingers tighten around my arm again and he opens his stride. "Ow, you're hurting me."

"Don't tell me you don't like it." He stops and yanks me against his side, looks down at me. His lips part, dark lashes lowering over his eyes. He draws an uneven breath. "Dammit, you smell good. Always smelling like sugar and roses... I remember how you cried out as you came, every sound you made. I remember your tits, your pussy, your mouth."

Jesus. Why am I turned on by his crudeness?

It's not just that, though. In the dawning light, he's almost inhumanly handsome, a delicateness in the high cheekbones and the long-lashed eyes that contrasts with his hard, masculine jaw and wide mouth.

I remember them, the Twins, saying that they don't know who is the changeling and who his human counterpart. I remember Tink suggesting the changeling was Wes, the blond, tawny-eyed hottie, but now I'm not sure.

No wonder the parents couldn't tell, either.

His scent winds around me, smoky and heady. His other hand slides around my waist and rests against the small of my back, pressing me to his muscular body, strong and unyielding. It's so easy to lose myself in him, not to care anymore if this is real or not.

He bends his head and kisses me, his mouth hard on mine, his tongue parting my lips only to slide inside.

He kisses me, assaults my mouth, conquers it, and I gasp when I feel him hardening against me, that steel rod of flesh pushing against my belly. It's harsh and demanding, that crush of lips and teeth and tongue, possessive, and it sends an ache between my legs, a heaviness that needs relief.

And then a sharp pain in my lower lip makes me jerk back, breaking the kiss. Panting, confused, I stare up at him, waiting for it to make sense.

"... did you just bite me?" I breathe, probing the inside of my lip with the tip of my tongue.

"You asked if I'm real."

I slap his chest. "You could have pinched me. Nobody asked you to bite me."

He smirks. "You taste good. And you liked it. I can smell your arousal, you know. It smells like honey cake with candied fruit."

Shit. The ache between my legs is getting worse.

I'm wet. For him.

And he knows it.

"How could you smell that?" I whisper. "Are you the changeling after all? I bet humans don't have such a sense of smell."

He regards me from half-slitted eyes that glow like burning coals. "Perhaps."

I open my mouth to ask why he hasn't said so before, why he agreed with Wes that they don't know who is who, when another familiar voice reaches us.

"Hey, Colt! Come over here." Wes appears, his hair a golden halo, coming toward us. "What are you doing? Did you find anything?"

"Yeah." Colt snickers, and his teeth look oddly sharp in a brightening light, a little like Tink's had that time he'd bent over me. "Yeah, I found something all right."

"I beg your pardon," I mutter. "I'm not a something. I'm a somebody."

Wes comes fully into view and stops, staring at me, brows rising. "*Wendy*?"

"In the flesh," Colt says.

"Hi, Wes." I take him in, from the tousled blondness of his hair, his pretty eyes and handsome face to his powerful body, low-slung blue jeans and a black shirt with a few buttons undone, baring his strong collarbone.

"Well, well." Wes whistles, eyes growing heavy-lidded, a crooked grin on his face. "Look who's here. Peter said he wasn't sure he'd convinced you, and yet I see Colt already got his hands on you."

"Fast gun," Colt says and blows on his raised forefinger, as if on an imaginary gun.

Heat spreads on my face. "We only kissed."

"Hm. Did you, now?" Wes steps closer, gazing down at me, his mouth twitching. His golden eyes burn like moon crescents under his lashes. "Wanna show me exactly what you did with my brother?"

"I thought you said he's not your brother," I breathe, resisting the urge to step back as he crowds my space, his height and the breadth of his shoulders sort of dwarfing me.

It's not an unpleasant feeling. Like with Colt, it's exciting.

"He's not my brother," Wes says. "I just call him that for laughs."

"Really." I don't know if to believe him, believe either of them.

I'm annoyed at them for teasing me like this about something so important—and at the same time, I realize... I missed it.

How can you miss something you've barely experienced? Something you're not sure you enjoy or dislike. This banter, the way insults and teasing fly between them.

It's like... they're friends, all of them. Good friends, despite their arguments and the small acts of violence they practice on each other.

And on me.

Does that make me part of the family?

Does it matter? Is it crazy? Everything and everyone seems to be mad here. It's like some twisted version of Alice's Wonderland and I've fallen down the rabbit hole...

8

WES

Wendy...

I'd given up on ever seeing her again, given up on the hope of being saved but also of that odd feeling in my chest when I'm around her, that soft, velvety emotion—and now she's here and the feeling isn't soft or velvety anymore but rough and wrenching and almost sends me to my knees.

What's this? What *is* it? What is she doing to me?

It's all I can do not to grab her and enfold her in my arms.

That's not something I do. The hugs I tried to give Tink were always met with kicks and punches, and with the others, well... they're not the hugging type, either.

With her, I feel... I feel as if I can put down my guns and blades, close the distance and touch and be touched.

She is the one who is soft and velvety, smelling of roses and sweetness, like a dream from a past I barely recall, a time of safety and happiness—now mixed with heat and the razor-sharp edges of desire.

How can she tie the two together? Desire has always been violent. Truth is, everything has, for as long as I can remember, making violence the one thing I'm most familiar with. But she's different. She opens windows into memory, bringing back gusts of innocence and brightness, and *fuck...*

I don't know what to do with that.

From the look on Colt's face, neither does he.

"Whatcha staring at?" Colt mutters, and I know he's as confused as I am. "That's right, she's back. Think you can keep your dick in your pants for five minutes until we tell Peter about it, or are you gonna rut with her right here, in the dirt?"

I lift a single brow. "You mean, like you were doing when I interrupted you?"

"It was just a kiss," she says again, blushing, and it fucking kills me that she blushes after everything we've done to her, after she enjoyed all of it. It's like she thinks it's bad that she likes it, that she isn't sure why she's come back.

Any sensible girl would think that way. Any girl would have run away screaming and never returned.

It kills me that she doesn't realize how fucking thrilling it is. How sexy she is. How fucking arresting. She has a grip on me no other girl ever got.

We're sick bastards and she's the only girl who still seems to... *like* us, somehow, and that's not the whole of it.

Because we like her, too. Way too much. I see the way Colt looks at her. He was a cranky bastard while she was away, crankier than ever before, which is saying something, even with this new, precarious grip on life as the island shrinks and the monsters multiply, and now...

Now he's grinning like an idiot.

And it makes my chest feel tight and warm.

Goddammit.

This girl, these guys... After living with the Lost Boys for so long, hiding as best I can how I fucking *feel* about them, this girl, this Wendy comes along and the feelings only got *more.*

More intense, more real, more out of control.

Soon I'll burst with them like an overripe balloon and die.

Feelings can kill you.

At least here they can.

"Let's go," Colt says and I realize I've been staring into nothing for a while.

Nodding, I turn to go, jealous of his hand on her, of her kiss on his lips.

See? These things can kill you. Or get you killed. Like I said.

It's obvious the moment the Reds attack.

———

"WATCH OUT!" COLT YELLS.

That's my first clue that something's wrong.

Torn from my thoughts, it takes me a minute to gather my wits and realize what is going on.

Thinking is just as deadly as feeling. Thinking on this island is a luxury we don't have anymore. Nothing makes sense anyway, and taking the time to analyze things means less time to react.

Colt shoves me out of the way and lifts Wendy into his arms. "Reds!" he howls. "Run!"

Reds.

"To the camp," he says. "Oh shit, Tink. Fuck!"

"The other way!" I shout and grab at him, hauling him in the other direction. "Come on."

He frowns as if he doesn't know what I'm talking about but follows gamely. He's my other half, my mirror image, my shadow, and we do things together.

It's the way it's always been—except for the many years he was gone to the other side.

The fact I didn't age more than him while in the human world is a mystery, but it's always overshadowed by the ache I felt, the hole in my chest, when he wasn't there.

And the fact I now feel the same way about all of them is... just impossible.

Fucking nuts.

"Duck!" Colt yells and I duck as a missile whizzes over my head. A rock? "Fucking hell."

I couldn't agree more.

And here I go again, getting caught up in thoughts like an insect in a spider's web.

"We circle around!" I let go of Colt, trusting him to manage on his own, even with a terrified Wendy clinging to his neck—and I shouldn't resent him for that right now, shouldn't be wishing it was my neck she clung to, as we run for our lives—as we make our way away from camp, toward the beach.

Which, as it occurs to me belatedly, might not be the best fucking idea.

"Watch out!" I swerve, grunt when something hits me—an impact I feel deep, jarring my bones—and stumble.

"Fuck, since when do they have guns?" Colt hisses.

"Guns?" I whisper. "What the hell?"

The mindless monsters are now armed? Since when? Could things get any fucking worse?

Wait, don't answer that.

I take two steps and waver, my balance off. Jesus Christ, what do I do?

"Wes," Colt whispers and Wendy's voice echoes my name, a sweet answering call.

"Go," I hear myself say as if from a distance, fumbling at my belt to pull out my gun. "Run!"

"No fucking way," Colt says.

"Put me down," Wendy is saying, "Colt, put me down right now—"

"Wendy!" Peter comes running, his knives twirling like burning stars in his hands. He throws one, then the other at the

Reds, and keeps running, heading for us. "Wendy, think away their guns!"

"What?" she asks, her voice a breath. "What do you mean?"

"Whose face are they wearing? Whose gun are they shooting?" Peter reaches my side, grabs my arm and hauls me to my feet. He slings my arm over his shoulders. "Come on, let's keep moving."

"My... my father's," she whispers, as Colt pulls her along, and we race toward the ruined city, which is a fucking bad idea, I'm sure of it even as my thoughts grow fuzzy and blurred.

"Change them, Wendy. Change them now!" Peter shouts. "Put a different face on the Reds. A friendly face."

Her next breath sounds like a sob. "I can't..."

"You can do it! This is your dream. Your nightmare. But you're awake, you're conscious. Do it!"

"It's not that easy!" she shouts, then yelps when Colt scoops her up again and overtakes us. "I don't know how to do what you say!"

Maybe she can't, maybe she's not the one—and back to the meandering thoughts. They're more confusing now, spiraling into dark wells and bursting into fountains of stars.

"Stay awake, Wes!" Peter shakes me. "Stay with me."

"I'm right here," I slur.

Why the fuck am I slurring? My feet drag, stumble over one another. Fuck, I'm tired.

"We won't make it," Colt says, turning and shooting at the Reds. Bang, bang, his bullets fly.

I haven't managed to even draw my gun yet. My hands are shaking. My entire body is shaking.

"Wes, no." Peter shakes me again. Or maybe I'm the one shaking him. "Wendy, goddammit, put a stop to this hell!"

"How?" she wails, squirming in Colt's hold as they run ahead of us, her face streaked with tears. "I can't! Peter, I can't!"

My breathing echoes strangely in my ears. I'm so cold.

Colt is right. We won't make it. We're heading straight for the Reds' stronghold to keep them away from Tink, but once we're inside the town we'll be butchered.

The end to a centuries-long struggle to save Neverland and ourselves.

Just like that.

My knees for some reason buckle and won't straighten. I'm dragging Peter down with me. He's cursing. I wish I had enough breath to curse along with him. The world is fading.

Colt is shouting something I can't make out.

Then we stop.

"Peter," I breathe. "Go. Go!"

He doesn't move, his arm wrapped tightly around me, pulling me back upright. "What in the holy fuck," he whispers.

I lift my gaze. My eyelids are leaden, and the sight that greets me doesn't make any fucking sense, even as the sounds of fighting reach my ears.

What the hell.

An army is fighting the Reds, swords and knives flashing, an army of men, and leading them...

Hook.

The fuck?

He fights like a demon—or an angel—white-blond hair flying, powerful body moving with confident strength, his sword, similar to Tink's but longer, flashing like lightning.

Slumped against Peter, I watch him lead his men against the monsters, heedless of bullets and claws and fangs, slashing and cutting a swath through the enemy.

Only I thought *he* was the enemy, too... So damn baffling...

His shadow fights apart from him, behind him, so he's like a two-backed beast—a grin pulls at my mouth, not even sure why — and his eyes glow as he twists and turns. He's using his sword like an extension of himself, a two-handed grip on the handle, a fight that looks like a dance, and dammit, Hook—*Jas* —is damn gorgeous.

Always was.

Seeing him through the haze that had settled over my vision, I hurt for not having him with us.

"See? He likes us." I try to elbow Peter, forgetting I'm leaning against him with all my weight.

Peter says nothing.

The battle goes on and on, and then suddenly it's all over, the remaining Reds turning around and fleeing.

The quiet in the aftermath has an unreal quality.

"Jas," Peter whispers as Hook lumbers toward us, wiping blood off his face with his forearm, his sword dripping crimson. He has a cut over one brow that's bleeding sluggishly, painting half his face red, like a mask.

"Fisher King." Hook stops in front of Peter, his gaze raking over us. "And the Lost Boys. Oh, and Wendy. Fancy meeting you all here, on this ever-shrinking island. Will wonders never cease."

"Stop joking about. You saved us," Peter says slowly, as if the words feel weird in his mouth. "From the Reds. *Why*?"

"Trust me." Hook is breathing hard. He rests the tip of his sword on the ground, leans a little on it. His men hang back. Well, not men, not really. They are shadows, flickering in the brightening morning. As the island shrinks, so does their reality. "Just trust me, Peter."

"First, you attacked Wendy in the real world," Colt says, jerking her against his side, "and then you sent her back there, and you expect us to trust you?"

"I never attacked her," Jas says. "I was only going to stop you from taking her in the first place. And I sent her back to protect all of you."

"Protect them from whom? From me?" Wendy asks, sounding indignant.

"Your nightmares are getting worse." Jas nods at the bodies of the Reds. "Case in point. The monsters have become more powerful."

Her brows go up. "But..."

"Come on," Peter says, gesturing with his free hand at Colt and Wendy. "We have to get back to Tink."

"Where *is* Tink?" Wendy glances around as if she's just noticed his absence. With everything going on, I hardly blame her, and ah *shit*, the world is darkening again.

Peter's hold on me tightens. "Hold on, Wes. Come on, let's check on Tink. He must be having kittens by now. And don't you even think about following us, Jas."

"No gratefulness." Hook sighs. "How the world has changed."

"Peter," I try again," what if Jas..."

"...Jas has his reasons for everything," Peter says. "Selfish reasons. And it's not Tink I'm so much worried about. It's you."

9

WENDY

Inside my head reigns chaos.

This is definitely not a dream. My lip still throbs where Colt bit me, though that's a distant sensation now. His renewed grip on my arm is bruising. The coppery scent of blood on the air is so strong I almost taste it, slickly sweet, turning my stomach.

The flight through the woods with the Reds behind us is a hazy memory that is sure to return in my dreams to haunt and torment me, but right now all I can see is the blood on Jas's handsome face, crimson running down his cheek, down his neck, down his sword.

All I can see is Peter hauling Wes along, Wes whose jeans are soaked in more blood, while next to me, Colt is vibrating like a live wire, his grip on me like a vise.

And Tink? Why isn't anyone telling me why Tink isn't here?

I'm so shocked by the mayhem greeting me upon my arrival at the island that I can barely sort through my thoughts or feel my feet.

When I stumble again, Colt wordlessly pulls me against his side again, wrapping his arm around me. A thoughtless gesture, feeling so natural, sending a wave of warmth through me, and I have to remind myself that this is the guy who pushed his gun into my mouth and left me tied to the bed.

The guy who used his dick in the same way later on.

And damn if my body doesn't react to the memory again.

Arousal isn't what I need right now. I wasn't even aware my body could get aroused after the repeated shocks and after running around the island for what feels like days but cannot be all that long. I'm just not used to it.

Not used to any of this.

The jarring shifts from world to world.

The gorgeous boys around me, touching me, holding me as if they don't want to let go.

The danger, the strain and worry and uncertainty.

I had built my life to be straightforward and simple, with clear goals: get a job, save money, bring my brothers to the city. Simple on the surface, but what lurked underneath?

"Face your fears."

Which fears? I think about that as we make our way through the sparse vegetation, following a once concrete path that is now broken in places and overgrown with weeds, the sky arching in a blue dome over us. I don't have any concrete fears. I'm a normal girl living in the city, trying to make a living and find her way, except that...

That I need my brothers out of the house.

Why? Why is it so important? What's the problem with them staying behind?

Colt comes to a sudden stop and I'm wrenched from my thoughts when a voice snaps, "Who's there?"

"Tink. That's Tink's voice." I pull away from Colt and he releases me with a small grunt, probably caught by surprise. "Tink!"

"Wendy, wait!"

But I'm running toward the source of the voice, Peter cursing behind me, calling for me to stop.

And then I see him, I see Tink propped against a tree trunk, sword in hand, his hair copper and black, his eyes huge and dark, his lips pulled back in a snarl.

I'm not sure he recognizes me, I realize as I launch myself at him, maybe that's why everyone behind me is cursing a blue streak—but as I put my arms around him, the sword drops from his hand and he slides down the trunk, taking me down with him.

One of his arms comes around me and he buries his face in my neck. His voice is unsteady when he whispers, "Wendy. You came back."

"When they didn't want to tell me where you were, I thought the worst, I thought..." I struggle to breathe past the knot in my throat. "I thought maybe you were dead."

"I'm as good as." His eyes are feverish when he finally lifts his head, his cheeks flushed.

The knot expands, cutting off my air. "Why?"

"Mermaid poison."

"No, Tink... No!" I turn my head to find the others gazing at us. "Peter, tell me how to cure him!"

"We can't," he says, his voice low and yet harsh.

"What? No. You can't be serious." I swallow hard. "You can't be... And Wes?"

"What about Wes?" Tink stirs, shifting with a groan and stretching out his legs. "Where is he?"

"He's hurt," I say, my voice thick. "The Reds shot him."

"I must be hallucinating," Tink mutters darkly, his cheeks turning ashen. "I thought you said the Reds shot him."

"They did. And then Hook and his men saved us."

"Then I'm sure I'm dying," Tink whispers. "I must be. None of this makes a lick of sense." Tremors are going through his strong frame and I stroke a strand of dark hair out of his face.

Black veins seem to pump under his pale skin, in his neck and at his temples. "None of it makes any fucking sense!"

"You're not dying," I tell him, shaking my head. "Wes, either. I won't let you. Any of you."

"And how will you stop it?" Peter is looking at me intently, Wes still half-hanging off him, his face kind of gray. Peter's blue eyes blaze.

"I'll figure it out," I breathe. "Give me some time, and I will."

I just hope time is on my side.

———

I'VE HELPED WRAP UP WES' SIDE AS BEST I CAN TO STOP THE bleeding. Now he and Tink are lying by the fire, asleep or passed out, Colt looking over them. At least that's what he seems to be doing, sitting there, frowning at the jumping flames as if lost in thought.

Outside the circle of the fire, in the thick of darkness, there's the red flare of a cigarette. I watch as Peter pulls a last drag of smoke and throws the cigarette down, steps on it, his face shadowed. My silver thimble glints against the hollow of his collarbone.

Seeing it on him is strange and yet feels right.

I walk over to stand beside him, wiping my bloody hands on my black jeans, feeling exhausted and frankly too tired to be nervous. "Peter."

"Who are you?" Peter asks, turning toward me, blue eyes narrowing. "Wait... don't tell me."

"Not this again," I whisper, shocked. "You can't have forgotten me."

"Never overestimate my memory. You're a Wendy, obviously."

"Wendy Darling," I snap. "Peter—"

"Yeah." His gaze flicks at me, bright, and his mouth lifts in a crooked smirk. "I was fucking with you. I actually remember who you are. Which is... troubling."

"Really?" I'm both relieved and annoyed at him. "Why?"

A shake of his dark head. "Since you came back, it's as if my memory reset and isn't as bad anymore. I assume it's your doing. You're the first Wendy who came back."

"To be fair, as I understood it," I mutter, "no other Wendy has ever left the island."

He tips his chin. "True, too."

"But I haven't done anything differently."

"Except *return*." There's a note in his voice I don't know how to read. "Except holding onto my acorn, except being *nice* to us." Now he almost sounds angry. "Why did you return, Wendy?"

"You said you needed my help."

"And why would you care at all?" he demands, dark brows knitting. "I mean... you've met us. Are you stupid?"

"You won't get a rise out of me like that," I whisper, then gasp when he slides his hand around my neck, cupping my head, hauling me closer.

"Are you an idiot, coming back to this?" he asks. "To four violent assholes who only wanna fuck you and use you for their own salvation? Fucking you, hurting you, dragging you around and barely stopping the monsters from getting you, ripping you away from your quiet life to make you face your nightmares on an island that's falling into the sea—"

I struggle against him. "Shut up!"

"Are you so starved for affection you'll take any scrap, any caress, any pleasure? Are you so desperate that you'd think you have feelings for us, that you're worried about us, that you—"

"Stop it!" I shove at his chest but he doesn't budge. His mouth is curled in a cruel smirk. "Just stop."

"What is it, did your daddy and mommy not shower you with enough attention? Well, newsflash, princess, you're not the only one who had a shitty childhood, so whatcha gonna do ab—"

I scream.

And scream.

The sound rips through the air, deafening, much louder than it has any right to be—and there's a crash.

The trees around us... vanish. They are gone. Not... crashed but gone, as in... there's flat earth. Black earth.

And...

"Wendy. Wendy!" Strong arms around me, hauling me against a hard chest, spicy male scent and quick breaths, a pounding heartbeat. "It's okay. It's okay."

My own heart is slamming around inside my chest. "Peter..."

"You really have the power," he breathes and eventually draws back, just enough to gaze down at me, his blue eyes wide. "Jesus on a stick. I'm sorry. Damn."

"You did this on purpose?" I whisper. "You pissed me off to see if I would react?"

"Yeah, though I really do think it was a stupid move on your part to come save a bunch of jerks like us." His smirk returns. "But hey, it's also stupid of me to even feel..."

"Feel what?"

The smirk falls. "Nothing. Nothing, shit. Thank fuck, though, thank *fuck* you came. No matter what."

I stare at him, at the emotions passing like clouds behind his eyes, and wonder what he had meant to say, and what he had really intended, and what... what he wants.

From me.

If it's the same thing I would like from him.

If he wants anything more than for me to somehow magically save this island—and from what? and to what end?— or if this strange power I seem to have is all he cares about.

I wonder if I still want the same, after he prodded the most painful parts of me. Starved for affection, he said, and it brings to the fore emotions I hadn't realized I had buried so deep inside of me I had forgotten they were there.

Now they're crawling up to the surface, cutting me up inside.

I'd take a bruising grip and a rough fuck over this painful digging up of feelings from the past, of images I thought had faded.

Pulling back, I turn around and head over to the fire. I think he breathes my name, but I don't stop.

Was coming back here the worst idea ever?

10

WENDY

"He isn't doing well," I whisper, stroking sweat-soaked blond hair out of Wes's pale face. "That wound doesn't look so good."

Infection, probably. And I'm not sure whether he's hurt something inside that would require surgery in the human world.

Grief is welling up inside of me, even though I tell myself it's stupid, just like Peter said, that I'm stupid for caring.

Wes mumbles something, lashes fluttering.

"He says he's glad you're here," Colt says.

It makes my eyes go hot.

"This is all my fault," I choke out. "If I hadn't come back, he wouldn't have been hurt."

"Don't say that." Colt throws a twig into the fire and gets up. "We are getting overrun. No more spaces to hide on what's left of the island, and the Reds are changing again. Meanwhile, the mermaids are crawling through the woods and the cliffs are crumbling into the waves. It's only a matter of time before they get us all."

He kneels down beside Wes, hunches over him, a hand pressed to his side as if he feels the wound on his own body.

Like a twin brother might.

What's the relationship between a man and his changeling other? How can they wear practically the same face, albeit with different colors, the same body but with different scars, and not feel connected?

When they fuck a girl together, do they enjoy it more?

Why am I even thinking of that now?

I glance sideways at Tink who's lying on the other side of the camp, Peter crouched down beside him, talking to him quietly.

Getting to my feet, brushing dry leaves and dirt off my denim-clad knees, I walk over to them.

"I said I'm dying," Tink is saying, a note of exasperation in his voice, "but I'm not dead yet, all right? Stop making plans for me. Make your own."

"I'm not letting you die, Tink, hear me?" Peter sounds like he has trouble keeping his voice down. "No way."

"Why, because I saved you and I'm dying instead?"

"That's not why and you know it. I..." Peter rubs the back of his neck. "Dammit, Tink. I'm... I can't let you go. You can't go."

A huff of laughter from Tink. "What's that, King? Are you catching feelings?"

"No. *Yeah.* I just... Fuck you, Tink."

"That's more like it." Tink sounds tired but satisfied, his voice going threadbare. "Not taking you down with me, asshole."

My heart clenches. Do they even hear all the emotion echoing in their words? Do they get what the other is really saying or are they that oblivious?

After all, they are guys. Guys are oblivious by definition.

Which is why Charlie always said one needs to grab them by the lapels—if they wear a shirt, that is—and kiss the fuck out of them or slap them, accordingly, to make them see the truth.

If only I could do that with myself... Make myself see...

For the first time in my life, I don't know what I'm feeling, and it's so frustrating.

Does wanting to slap a guy or four and then kiss them and make out with them sound unclear to you? Because it does to me. Twisting up my mind into strange shapes, bright echoes of a darker past that suddenly seems to be full of holes.

'Face your fears.'

"Wendy." Tink is looking past Peter at me. "You okay?"

Trust him to be concerned about my welfare when he's the one lying poisoned on the ground, with no antidote. His pretty eyes aren't dark as they had been earlier this morning but they're bloodshot. There's a dark track running down his cheek, as if from a tear.

A red track as if he wept blood.

With a sharp breath, I step back.

I can't.

Can't do this, feeling so lost and helpless, afraid that my return has brought nothing good, that they expect me to save them when I don't even know how to save myself.

"Wendy, wait." Peter comes after me and I stiffen.

The few winks I caught by the fire as the morning turned to noon haven't done much to dispel the weariness and the sense of foreboding that haunted my dreams.

I lift my chin, regardless. "Going to tell me again how I have daddy issues?"

"Did I touch a nerve?" He smirks, lifts a hand to rub his eyes and I try not to stare at his bulging biceps. This boy is *built*.

And still an asshole.

"My dad is none of your business," I mutter.

"I beg to differ."

"Peter—"

"Denial isn't just a river in Egypt." His voice is a soft growl and he's again standing way too close, right inside my personal space.

His presence is raising every small hair on my body, making me more aware than ever that I'm a woman and that he's a man, a violent, aggressive male, primal and savage.

Hot.

"I'm not in denial," I whisper.

"Look at me," he says, his big hand cupping my face, a thumb smoothing over my mouth. "Tell me again that you don't know what I'm talking about. Your nightmares shaped this island and its monsters. Tell her, Colt."

I jolt, having missed the approach of the dark-haired man. His hair has come loose around his square-jawed face, softening it. He reaches for me, and now I have the two of them touching me, Peter's hand still on my face, Colt's on my waist.

Colt's dark gaze moves from my eyes to my mouth. "Wendy," he breathes. "Only you can heal Tink and Wes."

"Stop expecting miracles," I snap, suddenly afraid of their expectations. "I can't."

"Why?" Colt's eyes are earnest. "You're here. That's a miracle all by itself."

I shake my head. "I don't know what you're asking me to do. Just a few days ago I didn't know you, didn't know about this place. I don't have magic. I can't wave my hands and perform healings or whatever else you think I can do."

"No need to wave your hands," Colt says. "Just... surrender. Let yourself remember."

"Remember what?" I mutter, exasperated, even as the holes in my memory pull like wounds. "What could I remember that might help you?"

"The Reds," he says. "Think about them. It was the first important change before you arrived here. They never had a face before, but the moment you stepped foot on the island, they acquired onc. Have you ever seen that face before?"

I start to shake my head again and stop, because that would be a lie. "Yeah. Their faces... seemed familiar."

"Did they?"

"Yeah."

"It's a woman's face," Colt says.

My breathing sounds shallow in my ears. "I thought at first it was my face they were reflecting but... it's not mine. It's my mother's face."

Peter curses softly. "Why, Wendy? What did your mommy do?"

"Don't..." I try to pull back. "Leave me alone."

"Can't do that, Wendy. Talk to us. You don't seem to get it yet: it affects us. Everything you went through affects us. Can't you see?"

Not possible. Why...? Why would it affect this place, this island... these guys?

Is this my escape? An escape in my own mind? Am I imagining this place, these gorgeous guys, violent and twisted as my subconscious probably craves them, to forget about reality, about my past, about my fears?

But I feel it, the connection. I see it. He's right. No matter how insane it seems...

"Come on, Wendy," Colt says. "Tell us."

"I told you before," Peter says. "Face your fears."

"I'm trying!" I take breath after breath to calm my pounding heart. "Trying, okay?" Trying to put the thought into words, the words into sounds. "My mom... she was jealous of me."

"Why was that?"

"Because my dad..." I swallow hard. "He paid me too much attention."

"Too much attention?" Colt repeats softly, a dangerous edge to his voice. "What the fuck, is that what I think—?"

"Not now, Colt," Peter cuts in, though his own voice is tight. His thumb moves soothingly over my cheek. "One thing at a time. She's letting us in. Don't interrupt."

"Are you letting us in?" Colt's hand slides up my spine to rest on my shoulder. "Are you, Wendy?"

"Yes," I whisper, the word, like my earlier confession, slipping out of me with some difficulty. It's like coughing up barbs. "Yes."

"Good. Then we'll reward you for being such a good girl," Peter says. And his other hand slides down to the front of my pants and pushes inside. "If you say *please*."

11

COLT

"Reward? she whispers, those pretty big eyes going even bigger in her small face so she's like a cute cartoon. Her curves, though, have nothing cartoonish about them. They're gentle, not too pronounced, and yet juicy.

Like her scent which is intensifying.

Do I sense a praise kink?

"A reward for every time you let us in," Peter says. "Every secret you share. Every attempt you make to erase the nightmare. But you have to beg for it."

I cut my gaze at him, questioning. After what she just confessed, can we just go on like nothing happened? Ignore what she has admitted to?

But her mouth trembles, her eyes dip to my lips, and if I judge from my life, my past, what she needs now are not kid gloves. She needs what we gave her before, and worse.

Much worse. It has to get worse before it gets good.

So we can make it better.

"How is that a reward then?" she whispers.

"You will come so hard you won't know what hit you," Peter growls, "I promise."

Her cheeks go bright red. Her lips part. She smells like summer fields and dark water, like sin and innocence, all rolled into one.

Peter chuckles softly, his body tensing ever so slightly, telling me he's getting hard at the thought. Maybe he was already hard when I came over, from touching her, from being close to her.

His hand trails over her cheek as he steps against her side, then he replaces his fingers with his lips.

She shivers.

Somewhere in the back of my mind are Tink and Wes, lying by the embers of the campfire, wounded and sick, fading away —but right now we have a sexy girl in our hands, a girl that seems to need gentling as much as we do, but differently.

A girl who needs saving.

Though as she turns in the circle of our arms, I think again that maybe it's not gentling she needs, but the opposite.

She needs roughness and manhandling, she needs her choices stripped away so she can crack wide open, slough off the thick shell she built around her.

And I need... I need her softness. Her submissiveness. Her willingness. Her slight resistance and faint moans, the fear crossing her eyes only to be replaced by thrill and excitement as I shove my hand deeper into her pants, into her panties, finding her small, hard clit, the wet, delicate folds of her pussy.

Peter holds her, sucking on her neck, as I slide my fingers through her slick heat, my breathing becoming ragged, my cock drilling a hole through my pants.

Without conscious thought, I pull out my gun, that extension of myself, and let its mouth kiss her back as I caress her from the front.

A small hiss escapes her, and that's when I realize that as if reading my mind, Peter has drawn one of his knives and is caressing her neck with the flat of the blade.

Her eyes are heavy-lidded, but her jaw is tense and I can see her pulse racing away under her skin.

Fear.

Oh yeah. That's what I'm talking about. I press the gun harder into the small of her back, push my fingers into her pussy, and she clenches, whimpers. *Damn...* I have to have her, take her here and now.

Peter groans, running the blade up, toward her jaw. "Don't move, girl," he breathes. "Stay still."

Another whimper.

"Mine," I growl, pleasuring her roughly, seeing her struggle as she tries to fuck herself on my fingers and at the same time restrained by the feel of my gun and Peter's knife pressed to her body.

"Mine," Peter echoes my growl. "I'm taking her first."

"No way in hell."

He breathes out. "Together," he offers.

I consider it. "Fine."

We don't ask her. We'll take our pleasure with her, and she'll love it. I know it when she moans at our words and starts to come, clenching harder around my fingers.

I pull them out before she's done.

"Colt," she starts, strangled.

"You come when I say so," I tell her softly, pressing my mouth to the shell of her ear, biting lightly, and I almost come in my pants when she breathes what sounds like "please," and "let me."

"You'll take both of us," Peter says.

She gasps and nods.

"I'll take her pussy," I say. "Peter, you get her ass."

"Oh, yeah. Want me to take your virgin little ass, Wendy?" Peter licks her neck where his blade has been. I can't see if he's broken the skin. "You've never done anything like it before have you? It will hurt. You know how big my dick is. Want it anyway?"

"Oh, God, yes," she breathes.

"And at the same time have Colt's dick fill your pussy? Fuck you hard? Can you take us both at once?"

Fuck.

She's trembling, and damn, this is what gets us off, what we've been weaned on. Violence. Fear. It's no big fucking wonder it turns me on, that it feels familiar and safe.

Will she still beg for it when we're done with her?

Will she still stay?

And does it matter when this world is about to end?

———

PETER IS LICKING THE BLOOD OFF HER NECK LIKE A VAMPIRE. HE won't kiss her, he's never kissed anyone, so I grip her chin and force her to break away and turn her head to kiss me instead. He shoves up her sweater to fondle her tits and I shove my gun into the back of her pants, over her ass, between her ass cheeks.

It's a constant tug-of-war between us.

Pulling away, I slip the fingers that had been inside her into her mouth. "Taste yourself," I say roughly, and she obeys, pupils dilating as she sucks on my fingers. "Fuck!"

My cock throbs.

Peter is already shoving her backward, undoing her bra, putting his mouth on her tits, and my fingers slip out of her mouth.

I'm breathing hard, dazed from all the blood flowing down to my dick, so I let Peter shove her up against a tree trunk and suck on her nipples as I gather my wits.

Then I holster my gun and grab Peter by the shoulder, push him aside.

"The fuck," he growls, all teeth, his shadow snapping at me like a rabid dog. "Get your hands off me."

And all that aggression sparks something in me—touching my King, the man I'm following, the alpha male of the pack who has been half-crazy for an eternity—and I crash my mouth to his.

A brief taste, a tussle, a savage bite and war for dominance as my tongue stabs his, then twines with it, Peter's grip on my arm bruising, his taste salty and bitter, fierce and heady—

We break apart, panting, lips throbbing.

Peter's eyes are wild, a mirror of my own.

Then as one, we turn toward our prey. She's watching us, eyes a little wide, her blouse still rucked up over her breasts, her bra pulled down.

Sinful.

Debauched, one would have said back in the day, back when I left the human world for this one. *Promiscuous. Easy.*

But I don't feel human, and I never cared for such labels. After all, what am I, then? A rake? A psycho predator? All that and more.

And she's so hot when she lets go, when she licks her lips, looking at us like *we* are the prey, not her, like she'd happily blow us, lick us, pleasure us. Take us.

In two movements, we push her down to the ground, on the litter of leaves and those stupid acorns Tink made us eat, and...

Pushing all thoughts of Tink and Wes out of my head, all my questions about Jas, about everything that's been going on, I pull down her pants and panties, all in one movement, leaving her bare, sitting on her ass.

"No more pants or panties," I growl.

"That's right," Peter chimes in. "I want easy access whenever I want to fuck you, Wendy. Skirts and no underwear from now on."

She gulps. Fuck, her eyes are black with need, her pussy rosy and glistening. Inviting. Delicious.

She's still wearing that sweater, rolled up almost to her neck. I grab it, pull it off her, needing to see her finally completely naked. Her blond hair falls in a tousled mess over her pale shoulders.

Peter lifts her to her knees, kneeling behind her, and runs his blade once more over her neck.

She gasps, leaning back against him, and her rosy nipples pucker, turning into hard points. My mouth fucking waters at the sight but I make myself wait, be still, as Peter puts his other hand between her legs, stroking her, spreading her slick cream to her ass, getting her ready.

She's gasping now, her cheeks bright red, the flush spreading down her neck to tits, her legs trembling where she's kneeling. I see the movement as Peter dips his fingers inside her pussy, then strokes back, between her ass cheeks.

With a low growl, I unzip my fly and pull out my dick. It's so hard I hiss as I wrap my fist around it. "Enough foreplay. Give her here."

"As if you know what foreplay is," Peter mutters, a grin in his voice. *Fucker*. He pushes her forward and her eyes widen in alarm. She punches her hands forward as she topples against me, and I grab her before she smacks into me, my dick trapped between us.

I lay back, dragging her over me, grinning up at her. "Feel me, baby? Ready for me? You had my brother before, and he's a pale shadow of what you'll get with me. Come to the original."

Confusion washes over her fine features. "But you said—"

"Forget what I said." I slide my hand between her thighs and flick at her clit, making her moan. Her hands are pressed to my chest, on my pecs, and her weight is slight yet warm and perfect.

My cock throbs where it's pressed against her belly.

Sliding my hands over her hips, I lift her just enough to allow my dick to rise, a little more, and the head aligns with her pussy.

The first shove into her is such fucking bliss I get dizzy. My groan echoes, bouncing from tree to tree as my dick pushes into tight heat. Teeth gritting, I shove deeper, dimly aware of her moan. She bows over me, her tits hanging, tempting, her mouth so close I could lick at her lips.

I hang suspended in the moment, a rushing sound in my ears, my hands back on her hips, holding her there.

With a whimper, she tries to move, rock her pelvis, and the hard tips of her nipples brush over my chest.

Holy fuck.

I stop her, keep her still as I focus on not shooting my load just yet.

Slowly I pull her down and curse as her pussy engulfs my dick inch by inch, tightening, taking more than any girl has before.

Can't be sure. All memories of other girls are fading the more time I spend with her. Is that normal? Truth is, I never paid those other girls much attention.

This one has all my focus. Has had it since she stepped foot on the island. And...

Fuck. I feel Peter push into her from behind, distantly hear her cry of shock, feel her shudder against me, feel her pussy clench, impossibly tight, squeezing the hell out of my cock.

Feel Peter's dick as it shoves into her ass, feel every fucking damn thing.

My back arches off the ground, my fingers digging into Wendy's waist, my balls unbearably full. "Goddammit!"

Peter's heartfelt cursing answers me as he thrusts deeper.

Wendy lets out a wail. She's biting her lower lip, cheeks crimson, rocking slightly on top of me, shaking. I wonder how it feels to have both of our fat dicks inside of her. I search her face for signs of anything—distress, pain, pleasure—but it's hard to read.

Struggling not to move, not to thrust until I'm sure Peter is all the way in, until I know she's okay, I'm caught by surprise when she rocks harder, clenching, moaning.

It's my cue to thrust up.

We all groan.

Then Peter thrusts, a counterpoint, and she gasps, throbbing and tightening around my length, scorching hot and so damn snug I can't breathe.

I want to lick her nipples, toy with her clit, play with her ass.

I want to feel where we're joined, where she's joined with Peter, but all I can do is thrust again, helplessly.

Never met a girl who could render me helpless, that much is crystal clear.

And then she says, "Use your gun." Her voice is breathy. "Caress me with it. Please... it means something to you, doesn't it? That gun. Something important."

"I'm not fucking you hard enough," I growl, "if you can string so many coherent words together."

But I pull my gun out of its hip-holster anyway because she's right, it means something to me, it turns me on even more, and the fact she asked for it... it's blowing my mind. That she wants to feel it against her skin... it's driving me fucking crazy.

I slide it between her breasts, the barrel like a finger gliding in the valley between the twin mounds, then over each breast, circling her nipples.

"Oh, yeah..." She moans. "Do it."

Holy fuck. Sharing this with her is everything. That she gets pleasure from it is *everything.*

That she might accept a sick bastard like me, like Peter... That she'd ask for it.

It's the stuff my dreams are made of, and she's real.

12

WENDY

Colt pulls out his gun and slides the barrel over my ribs, over my breast, over my nipple, and shit, I don't know why it makes everything sharper, every sensation more intense —his thick cock inside me, Peter's in my ass. That fullness I'm still coming to terms with.

I've never taken it up the ass before.

Never been with two men at once.

I've always been a good girl, always tried to be—bored and unsatisfied as I was, not knowing what I wanted, what I needed.

This is what I need.

The metal is cold against my heated skin, like ice, the contrast making the fire between my legs burn hotter.

My palms press into Colt's firm pecs as I rock my hips and moan, pleasure gripping me, the pressure below rising and rising, a molten magma core about to explode.

Colt's beautiful face below me is hazy, long lashes casting shadows on his high cheekbones, his dark hair fanned out on the leaves and soil, a puddle of black silk.

Distractingly attractive.

"Come to the original." Did he mean that literally? Is he the

human brother? Did he—?

Something cold slides over my neck, followed by the hot trail of Peter's lips. His cool blade. His warm mouth. Too many things going on at once, confusing my body, buffeting it on all sides, inside and out.

And Colt keeps thrusting up, into me, Peter sliding in and out my ass, their cocks so big it hurts to have them both inside and yet so pleasurable I never want it to end.

Except the pressure is mounting, inexorably, inescapably. My breathing echoes in my ears, my heart is racing, pounding in my temples, in my wrists, between my legs. Deep inside my belly.

The aching tips of my breasts drag over Colt's chest, over his coarse shirt, sending jolts straight to where I'm burning.

My breath is coming in small sobs, my chest is tight, my hips rocking as fast as Colt's grip on my waist allows, which isn't much, and Peter's hand on my waist is slowing me more, and I need...

More.

Faster.

Harder.

But their thrusts slow down to a crawl as if in silent agreement.

"Colt," I breathe. "Please. Peter..."

"Want to come?" Peter's blade slides down to my shoulder, a cold snake, a burning bite. "Tell me."

"Yes," I whisper.

"How bad do you want it?"

I shudder. "Peter..."

"Want to come?" Colt slides his gun over my other breast, teasing my nipple, and God, I ache. "Beg for it."

They like that. They like me begging for my release. And I'm so close, so frigging close...

"Please," I whisper.

"Please, what?" Colt breathes.

"Please, let me come. Please..."

"Goddammit." Colt puts the gun away, on the ground, and grabs both my hips to thrust up harder. "I love how you say it..."

Peter also seems to forget about the knife as he grunts and starts fucking me faster, the slip and slide in my ass feeling so good I forget how to breathe.

"Take it," he groans, "take it like a good girl."

And even though I'm not a good girl anymore, even though I'm only good at begging to be fucked, I almost come at their praise.

We're racing toward release, at last. Every punishing thrust pushes me closer to the edge, closer and closer still, until I fall with a cry, my eyes falling shut.

I shake with the force of it, pleasure erupting inside me, making me clench so hard it's almost like pain.

Like what's happening is a bigger explosion, a bigger conflagration than my release.

I swear the trees bend and twist, while I gasp and pant as wave after wave rolls through me.

I feel the moment the men follow me, one after the other.

First Colt, his gorgeous face twisting, his powerful body tensing, muscles bunching under my thighs and palms. Then his eyes fly open and his mouth goes slack as his cock jerks inside me. His shoulders come off the ground, and he curls up toward me, his hips still thrusting up.

Then Peter's teeth bite into my neck, the small pain washed away in the pleasure. He thrusts one last time, deep, and holds, body rigid and trembling at my back, his hands like vises on my waist.

Holy shit.

Wow.

I slump over Colt, my legs shaking uncontrollably, my arms, too, my body too lax and heavy to hold upright anymore. His hands slide around me in a loose hug, my head pillowed on his strong chest, while Peter curses softly, bowing over me.

I'm inside a hunk sandwich, and they're both still inside of me.

A small giggle escapes me. This is totally crazy. Between this morning and now, I've run from monsters, taken care of the wounded, confessed to old fears and traumas and to the fact that the monsters here wear my mother's face—and was then fucked by two of the sexy, psychotic men who inhabit the island.

And it's not even evening yet...

———

"What the fuck happened here?" Colt mutters, tucking his cock back into his pants and shoving long dark hair out of his face. He frowns.

"What?" I mumble. "What's wrong? Peter—"

Peter has a bruising grip on my wrist—of course—and is dragging me toward the fire before I've had a chance to even pull my panties back on. I'm only in my sweater and it barely reaches my hips. My bare feet crunch on leaves and twigs, and ow, tiny sharp pebbles.

I'm still dazed, lost in the afterglow of my release, leaking cum between my legs, and starting to feel how well I was used down below. As I stumble to a stop beside Peter, I still don't know what is going on.

Why Colt has fallen to his knees beside Wes.

But slowly fear trickles in, chilling me. "Wes? Did something happen to him? Colt, what's wrong?" I'm pulling away from Peter and instead of releasing me, he goes with me so that we are both standing over Wes and Colt.

The view that greets me is unexpected.

"I'm okay," Wes says. He has sat up and lifted his bloodied, ruined shirt, studying his flank. "I'm good."

His scarred but otherwise... not-bleeding, not-gaping open flank where I'd secured a tight bandage earlier, the infected wound with the puffy red edges that had sent a fever through his body, making it too hot to the touch, that had glazed his eyes.

The perfectly clear eyes that he now lifts at me.

He grins.

"How is this possible?" I whisper, grinning back without a conscious effort. "You're okay!"

"Looks like it." His golden eyes are earnest and serious, in contrast with the wide grin. "Wendy..."

Finally, Peter releases me and I go down on my knees beside Wes to touch his face. "I'm so glad!"

He lifts his hands to my face, cups my cheeks. "You did it."

"What do you mean?" I whisper, smiling and trying to read his gorgeous face. "I don't understand."

Peter is frowning down at us. Colt has a stunned expression on his face that would have been funny under any other circumstances, if only it didn't mirror mine.

"He means the mind-blowing, magical sex you had with them," Tink drawls, coming to stand over us, and I jerk back with a yelp. "Getting it now?"

"Getting what? Tink..." I slowly get up, tugging ineffectively on the hem of my sweater but too amazed to care that my bare crotch may be showing underneath. "Tink, you could barely stand before, how..."

"The mind-blowing, magical sex you had with us," Colt says, rising, too. His mouth is twitching. "Ain't that right, Tinkers?"

Tink huffs what sounds like a laugh. He's standing there, wearing a crooked smile, his hair streaked with pink and copper, arms folded over his chest. He looks... Stunning. Graceful. Arresting. Hot.

And *healthy*. Safe and sound.

"You..." I don't even know what to say. A thought occurs to me, making me freeze "Wait... Was all of this some sick prank? The both of you pretending you were dying, saying you were dying, just to make me believe it, and I don't know, *grieve* for you—"

"Would you?" Tink steps closer, gazing down at me with those emerald eyes of his. "Grieve for us?"

"Of course I would, what do you think? You..."

He unfolds his arms and reaches out a hand to touch my face, trace my mouth. "You would, wouldn't you?" he says, something like wonder in his voice. "You'd be sorry to see us go."

It's too much. Too confusing. I don't know what to believe. So I whirl on Peter. "Is this for real? Were they dying?"

"I thought so," he whispers, his face a little pale and... it doesn't look like he's lying. Come to think of it, I saw the way Colt had sunk to his knees beside Wes.

This isn't a theater. It isn't a prank.

"Then... did you know this would happen?" I demand. "When you..." I wave a hand. "Did what you did?"

"You mean, fucked you?" Colt says helpfully. "Both of us, at the same time?"

Heat spreads over my neck and face so fast it's like a wildfire. "Yes. That."

"I... have to admit that it's the first time in my long, long life that I hear of sex magic on the island," Peter says. "Or see it done. It certainly never happened with the other Wendies."

A shocking flare of anger washes through me, making my cheeks burn and my throat grow tight. "You did that with other girls before me?" I demand.

And then deflate because of course they did.

Why did I think I was special?

13

WENDY

Peter paces a little, back and forth, rubbing at his chin. "Could it really be the sex? What is different this time?"

"We've never wanted the other Wendies this much," Colt says.

"Point," Peter concedes.

That sure is gratifying, but... I'm not sure I want to hear any more about how they fucked other girls before me. "Which means what?"

"I dunno." Peter rubs the back of his head. "That you're the one?"

"How can we still not be sure about this?" Tink taps his foot and rolls his eyes. He's a bit of a drama queen. "I mean, look at us. She healed us. What more do you want to convince yourself?"

"You know what I want," Peter says. "What is coming. Yeah, I remember now, okay?"

"*What* is coming?" I ask, Tink's words echoing in my mind when he said, "*She healed us.*" "What am I missing?"

"The Night of Nights," Tink whispers, eyes darkening.

I blink. "What is the Night of Nights?"

"The end of the worlds," Peter says.

"Bullshit," Tink snarls. "The worlds won't end, no matter how much I wish…"

"You wish what, Tinkers?" Peter asks. "For an end to everything?"

He shrugs. "The end of dreams."

Peter grunts. "That can never happen."

"Can't it? Ever wonder who Wendy really is, why this island is fashioned after her nightmares?"

"A witch?" Wes mutters and I glance at him. He's brushing off the leaves from his pants, blond hair falling in his eyes. As if nothing happened. As if he hadn't been so sick half an hour ago.

"I already told you I'm not a witch," I mutter.

But how did I do this? Was it really me?

So yeah, what am I?

"It's not a matter of her having magic," Tink says. "It's a matter of her being linked to this place."

"And how did it happen?" I demand. "Why am I linked? Linked, how?"

"Every Wendy was linked to Neverland," Colt says quietly. "But to a lesser degree. We've never met one whose nightmares consume her, and can therefore change this place."

"It's not a matter of who you are," Tink says to me. "It's a matter of how much you fear."

"Tink has theories again," Colt says. "It's the same story every hundred years or so."

"It's different this time and you know it," Tink grumbles.

"Wait… just wait." I lift a hand to stop their bickering. "How can my fears save you? I don't understand."

"I don't either," Colt admits softly.

"Beats me, too," Tink says.

Awesome.

"How come…?" I frown, shake my head. "How come do

you, a half-Fae who has lived on this island for centuries with no way off it speak slang? Not current slang, mind you, but still…"

"Told you those movies were dated." Tink glares at Peter.

"Movies?"

"I brought him a DVD player and movies. But Tink…" Peter smirks. "That was some time ago."

"Outdated movies and hand-me-down clothes," Tink goes on, clearly on a rant, waving a hand in the air, "that's all I get every time you come back from the human world, when it's not bad enough that I'm a prisoner on this rock in the ocean like a castaway, and that there's not even a proper bathtub and that—"

"Tink."

"—you didn't bring us any new clothes and we lost everything in the waves and now I'll be stuck in these bloodied, filthy clothes forever unless you don't mind me going around buck-naked as I wash them, though why you should mind I don't know, I'm—"

"Tink. You know we still have a trunk full of clothes, right?" Wes says.

"Irrelevant." Tink huffs. "So, Peter Pan, what do you have to say for yourself?"

My brows have crawled up to my hairline. I turn to Peter who seems… embarrassed? He's grinning but his cheekbones are red.

"You're right," he says. "Tink is right. I didn't bring anything this time around, no clothes or food or weapons. I was…"

"Sick," I murmur. "You were sick."

He casts me a surprised look. "I was, wasn't I?"

"From drugs. You're an addict, Peter, at least in my world, or was that not real?"

"It was," he whispers. "I am."

"You take drugs in the human world, too?" Colt snaps. "Are

you serious? You go over there supposedly to find the right Wendy and instead you do Opium?"

"You're not watching enough movies," Tink says. "Opium is out of fashion. They have other drugs now."

"I don't do human drugs," Peter says quietly. "It's fairydust. I always take some with me."

"Why, Peter?" Wes asks. "Why, dude?"

"Why? Maybe because it's fucking hard being over there. You have no idea... Almost as hard as being here. This world... hurts my body. That one messes with my head. Leaving my shadow behind is a bitch, even if it's killing me when I have it."

Wes sighs. "Dammit, man."

"You don't get to judge," Peter says. "I'm the one who crosses over every time. Being over there on my own, trying to figure out what the fuck I'm supposed to do, how to survive while stalking girls, how to fucking kidnap girls and bring them over here to die... How the hell do you think I cope?"

"And here you cut yourself," I say and they all glance at me. "Just another way to self-harm."

Peter flinches. Casts me an annoyed look, eyes narrowed and flashing. "You mean like you did when you were younger?"

It leaves me floundering. "I... But..."

The scars have mostly faded. I used creams and oils and now you barely see the fine white webbing, but I guess it takes one to know one, doesn't it? I'm still staring at him, not sure if that's maliciousness in his eyes or sympathy. How can the two emotions look so alike?

"I think..." Wes says. "I think that world hurt you. It's why you came here in the first place. To escape, to make sense of it."

"No shit," Peter says, "I—"

"I wasn't talking to you," Wes says.

I blink.

Wait... was he talking to me? It was as if he was reading my mind, seeing my past, as if the conversation was with me, not Peter.

They have all fallen silent, looking at me.

Well, shit.

The silence stretches and stretches and I don't know what to do with myself under their knowing gazes when I can't read them, when I can't tell what they feel—and wasn't that always an issue, not being able to read my parents' faces before they did something, not getting a warning?

And then someone's stomach growls, breaking the tension, making it all… real and human again.

"Right," I say brightly, wiping my hands on my sweater. "With the talk about the end of the world and all that, I got hungry, too. How about some dinner?"

———

AS IT TURNS OUT, THE BOYS DIDN'T ONLY SAVE SOME CLOTHES before their home vanished but also food and plates.

Peter looks puzzled by this, scratching his head at the pile of dishes sitting on top of a tablecloth, along with some bottles of who-knows-what, some apples, and a heap of what looks like acorns. "Where did you get all this? Did the house sink slowly into the fucking ground, while you ran in and out snatching a full set of crockery?"

"We found the trunk in the bushes," Wes says. "No idea how it got there. And the dishes were inside the trunk, too. We gathered the apples and acorns. Tink told us what to look out for. Now we just need protein." He draws his gun, twines it around a finger. "Gonna go get us some."

"Wait." I take a step toward him. "You were on death's doorstep not half an hour ago."

"And now I'm not. See?" He winks. "Coming, Colt?"

"Yeah, yeah." Colt checks his gun and smirks. "Let's show those birds a good time."

Huh.

"Where do they get this endless supply of bullets?" I mutter as the two of them swagger away, still flabbergasted that Wes is fine—a miracle, only this is a nightmare island, so miracles shouldn't stick. "Do you bring them over from the human world, too?"

"Nah. I would never be able to bring enough. These are magical weapons, never running out of bullets."

"So there is magic here? I mean... I saw the mermaids and the Reds but the only person I saw actually doing anything remotely magical was Tink."

"And you," he says, a small frown on his face as if he's still trying to figure me out.

"We don't know that."

"Yeah, we do."

I kneel on the cloth, watching Tink who's gathering twigs for a fire, pink and copper hair sliding forward to hide his face, muscles bunching deliciously in his arms as he piles the wood in his hold. The soughing sound of the surf haunts my thoughts—like at the beach house, I think, all that time ago...

"I don't think it's the sex," I say slowly.

"Oh?" Peter is flexing his hands. I wonder if he wants to grab my wrists. I wonder why he isn't doing it.

"I think... it's admitting to things. Remembering things or rather... letting the memories back in."

"But you felt it, during sex, didn't you? That fucking roll of power that bent the trees over."

"I do but... I did have sex with..." I have to stop and swallow. "With Colt and Wes together, you know. And nothing happened. No power. No woosh of magic."

"I know," he mutters, "but that was before you returned. Returning changed something."

"Peter—"

"It changed... everything." He gives me a thoughtful look, but before I can ask what's on his mind, he grins. "I think we need to look into this sex theory more. Test it, ya know?"

I stare at him. "Who are you and what have you done with Peter Pan the Grinch?"

"Come here," he says and I obey.

PART II

"Boy, why are you crying?"
— J.M. Barrie, Peter Pan

14

TINK

Gathering a big bunch of twigs and broken branches, I crouch down and set about lighting a fire. Wendy is sitting beside the small pile of apples, talking with Peter about whether she was the one who healed us or not, whether she has magic.

My hands are shaking. To hide it, I busy myself arranging the wood in a neat pyramid. I can't... fucking can't keep up. For centuries it was only us, it was only the one purpose: find Wendy, fix the world, save it, and now...

Now there is confusion and uncertainty and more people and more variables and my body wants things it hasn't wanted in so fucking long I'd almost forgotten what arousal was, and...

The Night of Nights.

I had started to think it was a myth.

Just like the real Wendy.

Neverland is the shadowland, the fragments of dreams people don't want to remember. But a few people can change it so completely... or break it. Remake it.

I got used to the place. To the people. To the eternal

conflict. I liked the monotony of it. Frustrating as it was, the never-ending circle, it was also… damn comforting.

Now she's here, healing people, healing *me*. Changing the rules of the game. Hook is playing weird games, too, sending her back, saving us, Peter seems clear-headed for the first time in forever, and I…

I hate not knowing what I'm supposed to do. What the right course is. How to keep… keep the things that mattered to me. The people that mattered. Will she…?

Fuck.

He's cupping her face now, saying something too low for me to hear, crouched in front of her, both hands on her cheeks. He can't stop touching her.

Of course he can't, she's magical, and soft, and pretty and everything all of us want.

Sometimes I think I'm the only fucker who isn't sure he'd prefer pleasure over pain, the sharp tug of hope over the mire of despair and violence.

He hauls her onto his lap, and my insides clench and twist. Why can't I… What the fuck's wrong with me?

With a snap of my fingers, I light the fire, a little manipulation of the elements, a tiny draw that won't get the attention of the rulers of Faerie, and why do I still care? Why am I still scared? I should let it rip.

That thought is my cue to get up and stalk into the woods, so fucking mad and annoyed at myself and the world, the sounds of their joining following me, dogging my heels, her soft moans and his growly grunts as he closes his hand around her neck and thrusts his hips up, pistoning into her.

Why am I even feeling like this, this… mad, and itchy, and fucking devastated? It's not like I can join in.

And why is that, you'll ask?

Because I'm a fucking coward, a little broken boy in the

body of a full-grown man. Isn't it funny? So damn funny. Cracks me up.

No, that's a big fat lie. It *fucks* me up. Makes me feel half. Incomplete. Damaged. And I fucking hate it, even if it's true.

Violence is the only goddamn outlet I have, and my magic flares, a burning cold flame that shoves out of me, engulfs me. It ripples around me as I pull my sword and start hacking at trees.

Fuck that, and that other tree, and this tree in particular.

What the fuck, we need firewood anyway, and with every swipe of my sword, power gusts out of me, sending the leaves flying and the butterflies swarming in the air. Crows caw and black wings close in around me.

I stumble back a step, bowing over, my power raging—clawing out of me, clutching at the shadows nearby, sucking them to me. I have no shadow, and therefore I am a void, hunting other shadows, other shadows trying to attach themselves to me, like Peter's when he was away, like—

No. Stop. But—

I—my mind, my power—touch on a slippery, alien presence and recoil, then grab at it and *haul* even as I try to stop myself, but it's a lost cause. I am as I am, this black hole sucking others in. Half-Fae and full-out dangerous.

Cursing echoes in the woods, and dammit, there is only one person on the island with a shadow like that, my reason tells me. I grit my teeth, try to force the magic down, but it's not fucking working.

Only one person gave up his human shadow to be there, to work with the Fae who have no shadow. He was like me at first, back when he gave up his soul, and a shadow attached itself to him, a Fae leech made of thorns and spite.

Hook.

———

HOOK STALKS THROUGH THE TREES, THE TIP OF HIS SWORD dragging in the dirt behind him, his pale hair ruffled by an invisible wind, his eyes black like an animal's, flat and terrible.

I take a step back before I can get myself under control. Light coils around me. Light and dimness, light and doom, making my body shudder with every flare.

He's alone at least, not followed by the fading shades that normally follow after him, fighting his wars. His shadow forms a crown of antlers on his head, a garland with twin horns and a trail behind him like the dark tail of a comet.

The trees groan as he approaches, the leaves skitter down the trails. The branches bend away to let him pass. Pebbles and rocks roll out of his way.

Damn. I've never seen him alone before. Never seen him so untethered, so unleashed on the world, either. He's beautiful, beautiful like a deadly storm approaching, when you know you should be running away but stand still instead, staring.

And just as terrifying.

Fuck, I don't know what I fucking feel right now. If he decided to kill me, I'm not sure I'd fight him—but he takes a different tack, and now I'm probably going to kill him with my bare hands.

"Well, well, if it isn't the prettiest of the Lost Boys." Jas bares his teeth in a predatory grin that raises my hackles. "Hello, Tink."

Dark energy pulses around him. Seeing him like this, I can hardly credit the others' stories about him saving them from the Reds not once but twice.

Maybe he likes them. I doubt he likes me enough to save me, or leave me alone. I can't decipher the darkness in his eyes.

"Stay back," I demand, sending my magic swirling around me like a wall, a tower, a shimmering tortoiseshell castle. "Don't take another step."

"Always so skittish," he murmurs, slowing down, tilting his

head to the side. He has a bloody smear on one cheek. "How will you stop me, though?"

I glare at him. "Seriously? I can take you the fuck on anytime."

He grins. "I bet you could if you wanted to."

"What's that supposed to mean?"

"Maybe you don't hate me as much as you think," he says as if he means it.

"And maybe you're a delusional idiot. Just a thought."

No reply.

He circles me, oblivious to my magic.

It barely affects him anyway. Not only does the watch, the Mermaid Queen's token, protect him from the madness of magic, he's a creature of fey now, too. Has been for ages, and yet there is something tragically human about him.

I don't know if it's the sturdiness of his muscular body or the cut of his arrogant, gorgeous face, those big hands and big biceps and the big cock between his legs that I can only guess at from the way his pants hug his crotch.

Nothing delicate about Jas.

Not that Faerie has ever been a delicate place.

He reaches for me, that bastard, and turning, I slam my fucking magic into him.

A laugh escapes him even as his shadow roars, scarier than Peter's with its torn, distorted limbs, a sabertoothed monster with a deep dark gully ready to suck me down. Its long tail lashes around my ankles, burning cold, startling me.

"Now," he says, his breath brushing over my neck, making me shudder violently—and when did he get behind me again? "—where were we? Oh yeah. The pretty halfling."

"Pretty, my ass," I snarl and shove him away again. "Fuck off to your shadow buddies where you can play captain and tell yourself you're the good guy."

"You can't let a man touch you, is that it?" Jas says, a rasp in his voice. "Only a woman. Only Wendy. Am I close? Is it getting hot? You sure look hot."

Wendy.

I think of her dressed in her sweater, her thighs wet with the others' cum, her pussy peeking from underneath the hem.

I think of her in Peter's lap, moaning as he fucked her.

Damn, I'm hard. Have been ever since she came back, ever since the world seemed to go sideways—and that's saying something, given the sort of world I've been living in—and now this asshole is touching me and pretending to understand my mind when I don't understand it myself, for fuck's sake—

"Is that why you want her?" he goes on, undeterred. "Because she doesn't feel threatening? Well, think again. She's the most dangerous creature to ever set foot on this island."

"Fuck you, asshole." I give him the finger and a blast of my magic for good measure.

Still not affected. "Come on, Tink, fess up. Who hurt you?"

"Who hurt you, Tink? Who scared you so fucking bad? Tell me."

"Shut up," I growl.

He lifts his hands. "Haven't said anything. How about this: Peter saved you, or tried to, but you are still trapped, aren't you? Trapped with no way out and with all that pain—"

"Shut. Up!" My magic pulses, hot and cold, flames and ice. A sparkling carapace, deflecting questions and arrows, and I'm still stepping backward. "Enough. Goddammit, that's fucking enough."

Why is he digging inside my head?

He pats his sleeve. Vaguely, I notice that it's caught fire. "You've always been betwixt and between."

"And you are just a fucking pain in the ass and firmly on the other side, so what gives?"

"Didn't the others tell you?" he says. "I saved their asses."

"And what does that mean, huh? You're still against us.

What are you doing here on your own anyway? Looking for payment for your services? Get back to your fans."

"Fans." He chuckles. "Really, Tink."

"Power was what you wanted, so get back to collecting your victories. May the gods of Faerie give you what you wish for, you asshole. And to think... to think you were in love with Peter once, weren't you?"

"Who says my feelings have changed?" he asks softly. "For him? Or any of you?"

I ignore the small stab of pain in my chest at his words. *All lies*, I remind myself. *All fucking lies.*

"Who says it? I don't know." I shrug. "How about the battles you fought against him? Against us? That time when you almost killed each other? Ring any bells?"

"Love," he says, "is often close to hate. Or is it the other way around?"

"Goddammit, enough of your convoluted rhetoric. You sound almost like—"

"—A Fae? Like you?"

My breath catches. "I'm not—"

"—Yeah, I know what you are, pretty Tink."

A snarl rises in my throat. "If you call me *pretty* one more time..."

He laughs out loud. "Threats. Love it. Now, take me to Peter."

"... come again?"

"There is something he needs to know."

15

PETER

It's brutal and dizzying, this *want* for her. I take her just as brutally, hauling her on my lap and freeing my cock only to shove it into her, no foreplay, no games.

"Yes," she hisses, "yes, yes..."

She shouldn't like it so much. No other girl ever enjoyed my assholery. She shouldn't want it as much as I do...

It's too damn dangerous.

Makes me *feel* things. Softens my stone heart. Eats at it like water.

Can't have that.

So I fuck her harder, the silver thimble thumping against my collarbone. My golden acorn rolls between her tits, bright and blazing, blazing like my need for her. In counterpoint, I bite at her lip, cut off her air with my hand, grab her ass and squeeze hard enough to bruise.

And she comes, incandescent, robbing me of breath and reason, her nails digging into my shoulders, the slight sting shattering me.

I'm fucking undone. I swear my balls detonate like

grenades, my cock jerking inside her tight pussy, flooding her with my cum.

And all I want is more.

More of this.

More of her body in my arms.

Her taste on my tongue.

Her scent.

Her skin.

Her hair.

Her voice.

Her warmth.

I'm clinging to her and I should stop, push her away, but I fucking can't. Can't do it. Don't wanna push her away.

What the fuck, right?

And then two guys loom over us and I flinch, I fucking *flinch* because I was so distracted with thoughts and goddamn feelings that I didn't even hear them approach.

Worse still, I curl my body over hers to protect her.

From whatever these guys want.

"Peter," one of them says and I groan because I belatedly realize it's Tink, just Tink, and behind him...

"What the fuck," I breathe, curling over Wendy anyway, Wendy who is still impaled on my cock, which makes thrusting her behind me hard, pun intended. "What is *he* doing here? Have you lost your mind? Wait, don't answer that."

Tink rolls his eyes. "Don't tell me we got the drop on you? And you ask me if *I* have lost my mind? You were balls-deep inside her and shut out the world, did you? You can't keep your hands off her."

"Shut your mouth. We're all different around her," I say but what I mean is, *I can't stand how badly I need her, how I can't stay away from her, how you were right and I wasn't sure she was the one when I saved her life, when I brought her over. Because I didn't care.*

I wanted her for myself.

Tink was right. And it pisses the hell out of me.

"Sorry to interrupt," Hook says and wiggles his fingers at us. That asshole.

Looking fine like always. Frigging hot.

Fucking asshole.

"Now, before you say anything," Hook says, "I—"

"Tink, tie him up," I growl, lifting Wendy gently off me and hissing at the sensation of sliding out of her heat. "Dammit."

She moans, eyes heavy-lidded, gaze sliding from me to Hook and then to Tink and back.

Tink's cheeks color.

Hook smirks. "Wanna share? She's a pretty one, isn't she?" He glances at Tink. "You do like to collect pretty things. Pretty, broken things."

"Fuck you," Tink says because of course he takes it personally.

"I'd rather do it the other way around," Hook says, arching one pale brow. "Wouldn't you?"

"He's right," I mutter, "fuck you, Hook. Get off his case."

"Your wish is my command, of course." That damn pale brow is still up. "You can call me Jas, though. You used to."

"I used to do a lot of stupid things," I breathe.

"True," he says pensively, "you always were a bit of a hot-head."

"That's it." Hauling Wendy off me, keeping my hand on her wrist while my dick swings free, at half-mast, I lurch to my feet and pull my fist back to rearrange his handsome, stupid face. "I'm all out of fucks."

"Go on, then. Punch me," he says.

So I do, snapping his head to the side with a crack. My knuckles sting.

"Damn." He wipes blood off his lip. Smirks. "Didn't think you'd do it."

"Didn't you?" I snarl. "We've been fighting for centuries and you think I wouldn't punch you in the fucking face for having the gall to show up here like that?"

"And you're still a hot-head." He probes the inside of his cheek with his tongue. "Doesn't it seem weird to you that I came here like this?"

My grip on Wendy's wrist tightens until she whimpers. "You've always been fucking weird."

"Yeah." He nods. "There's that."

I relax my hold on her but not by much, because I fucking need to keep her close, or whatever the fuck. "But mostly an asshole."

"Anything else you wish to tell me?"

My nostrils flare. "Only with my fists."

His smirk falls. "Tuck your dick in, King, and let's talk."

"We got nothing to say."

"You'll feel differently after you've heard me," he says. "Hurry up, I can't linger."

"Minions waiting for you?"

"You have no fucking idea," he says slowly, viciously, "what it is like for me. So shut your piehole for once and listen."

It shuts me up. I want to yell at him that if his life is miserable, he brought it on himself, but something in his voice stops me. I nod at him. "Then talk."

———

WENDY HAS MANAGED TO ESCAPE MY HOLD WITH SOME EXCUSE about pulling on her pants, and though the thought of Hook—Jas—seeing her like that, half-naked and freshly fucked by me excites me, I let her go.

Seated on a fallen log, Jas is watching me with those bright eyes of his, while Tink fidgets, standing nearby, looking at anything and anyone but us.

"What did you do to him?" I finally ask.

"To whom?" Jas frowns. "*Tink*? You think I'd hurt him?"

"Come off it," I mutter, annoyed. "You'd hurt any of us. Have done so repeatedly. We're at war. Have you lost all your marbles? Think we're allies now because you fought off the Reds coming after us *once*?"

He sighs, a soft sound.

"What did we miss?" Colt and Wes walk into the clearing with two hares and a partridge. "Is it a war council?"

"Are we allies now? He did save us at the beach the other time, too." Wes nods at Hook. "Hey, Jas."

"We're not allies," I grind out.

"An enemy parlay, then?" Colt drops his haul on the ground beside the tablecloth with the dishes and fruit and wipes his hands on his dark pants. "Does he have anything on us so he can blackmail us? Hostages, perhaps?"

"Hostages." Hook sounds amused. "Why, is anyone gone missing? All seem to be accounted for."

"This isn't funny," Colt says, twisting his dark hair at the back of his neck. "Not after everything."

"See?" I say. "It's not just me. We all hate your guts."

"Do we?" Wendy, pants on and buttoned up, her hair a tangled blond mess and her cheeks still flushed, sits down on the cracked soil between myself and where Tink is still standing. She looks well-fucked and damn if that doesn't send a fresh bolt of desire down to my dick.

Down, dick. Not now.

"You don't know him," I mutter. "He's a sadistic prick."

"Because you're any different?" she breathes.

"Took the words right out of my mouth. A wolf knows a wolf." Jas is still smirking but it's starting to look strained. "We're all here, then? Good. Tink, won't you sit down?"

"Fuck off," Tink says between his teeth and goes to lean against a trunk.

Hook turns to look at the Twins who stand side by side, arms folded over muscular chests, twin expressions of dark suspicion on their faces.

I imagine they mirror mine. "You see, Jas? You're on wobbly ground here."

"Yeah, I see that," he says, looking down at his hands that hang between his legs. "I guess I deserve it."

"You guess?" I growl.

"Fine, you've made your point. You're right, okay?"

"Phew." I lean back where I'm sitting. "What a relief. I don't know what I'd have done if you hadn't agreed."

"Jesus," he says. "Okay. Listen up."

"You should hurry it up," Tink says. "Say what you came here to say and go. My fists are getting itchy to beat you up."

Jas's gray eyes flash when he looks up. "Violence breeds violence."

Tink leans forward, his voice a low hiss. "Then she's a fertile fucking little bitch, ain't she?"

"That's disrespectful," Wendy says, her light voice snapping like a whip, and Tink gapes at her.

"What?"

"Choose better metaphors," Wendy says and it's my turn to gape at her. This is the girl who shook with terror when she had first arrived on the island? This second time, it's not just the island that's different; it's her, too. Which makes perfect twisted sense. "Don't be a misogynist."

Tink blinks. "But you..."

"Yes, I like rough sex. That's a different thing. You don't get to diminish women." She sighs. "I can see this could be a long debate but I won't back off."

Hook is staring at her. Then he turns his gaze on me. "I like her."

"Get in line," I mutter.

Wendy stares at me, then she glances past me and jerks. "Peter…"

I catch a glimpse of Tink's face twisting and transforming, all teeth and black eyes, black wings stretching behind him, the fairytale gone and dead—before his magic lashes at me, sinking hooks into me, into my shadow. It jerks me to my feet and I stumble toward him, caught by surprise, yelling when my shadow rips itself off me and slides toward Tink.

"Tink," Colt shouts, "no!"

I sprawl on the ground, groaning, feeling like I'm bleeding from every orifice. Even my skin hurts. The sky spins above, white clouds and shards of blue. This is different from when I leave my shadow behind as I slip into the human world. It hurts but not like this.

I jolt—my shadow jolts—when Hook grabs Tink and shakes him, and he's monstrous, too, his shadow turning his white-blond hair into white spikes and scales, his face into a dragon's muzzle, his hands into claws.

"Stop it," he yells, "stop it, dammit!"

"Don't fucking touch him!" I haul myself back to my feet, grab Jas from behind, pull him back.

He reels in my arms. "Peter, something's off—"

"You bet your ass something's off." A darkness descends over me. "It's getting worse."

"What's getting worse?" someone asks. I think maybe it's Wendy.

Everything's getting worse. The spell. The distortion. It's this place. This nightmare. All the fears stitched together into one. Each other's fears feeding off one another. And Jas has been behind it all, coming here like a serpent to pry out information—

He tries to kick me, and his strength is a match for mine normally, but it's as if our combined power—the Lost Boys power—has him in a net. "No, Peter—"

"Here is where you pay for your crimes." I secure my hold on him, glance at the others. "Come on. I got him."

"What are you doing?" Wendy shouts.

"Meting out justice," I whisper, holding Jas as Tink comes at him and punches him in the stomach, as Colt lets his fist fly at Jas's jaw, as Wes goes for the ribs. "Take him down, boys."

It's a dark haze over us.

Inside of us.

The others' eyes are glazed, turned to animal eyes, all color, no white.

Tink is wearing my shadow like an ill-fitting suit, lashing out like he can barely control his fists, while the shadow shared between Colt and Wes changes shapes, forming one monster after another as they rain punches and kicks on Jas.

"No!" Wendy winds herself between them and us, her voice breathless. "Stop! Why are you doing this?"

"We're sadists, baby, I told you," Colt says. "We get pleasure from the pain of others."

"I don't believe that's who you are," she whispers.

"We're psychos," Wes says. "Didn't you notice?"

No, it's not like that. I'd have known. We're sadists when it comes to sex and pleasure, but we don't beat people up like this. Something... Something's off.

Wendy is right.

And she doesn't step back, doesn't shrink away from our madness.

"Stop, guys. I said, stop!" She shoves at Tink and the Twins and even through the weird haze I wonder if she's gone crazy at long last, if she wants to die as their shadows snap at her with fangs and claws. "Get back!"

And unbelievably, inconceivably, they do. They step back, and Jas lets out a long breath, slumping in my arms, his back to my chest.

His shadow melts into me, giving me a new jolt that rattles

my bones and the teeth in my mouth. I almost bite my tongue off when the power of that shadow pushes through me—also no foreplay, and dammit I'm a virgin when it comes to shadow penetration. My own shadow barely holds onto me at the best of times, or not at all, like now, when it's attached to Tink.

But I feel it when she kisses Jas. I feel it through him and his shadow, I feel it in my bones, that soft touch of her lips.

And want it.

The kiss that I've never had. It breaks me.

My thoughts start to grow fainter. Her face, her name, the feel of her under me—under us—and her voice in my head.

My vision goes black.

What a kiss it must be, I think as I fade.

A kiss to end all kisses.

A kiss to end the world.

16

WENDY

I don't know what possesses me to kiss Jas in the midst of this violence. The only thing on my mind was to protect him, stop them from killing him.

Why? I don't even know. I understand that he has been fighting them for a long time.

I also know he saved them, saved us more than once.

And yeah, that's confusing and he should really pick a side, but... seeing him pummeled like that, punch after punch snapping his head from side to side, blood coating his lips, running down his chin, I couldn't allow it.

Not when they seemed to have been possessed by something evil, something demonic and blood-thirsty, when Jas's shadow seemed to be fading, spreading thin, a cloud engulfing both him and Peter.

And then Peter falls to the ground, limbs loose, head rolling to the side, eyes closed. He's passed out, pale and still, and my heart wrenches inside my chest.

What have I done? What happened?

"Peter!" I scramble down on my knees, leaving a stumbling Jas to follow me. He thuds down beside me, goes down on all fours, blinking as I pat Peter's face. "Was he hurt before?"

"Did you and Peter kiss?" Colt says, grabbing Wes by the arm and hauling him back. They both seem a little dazed. "One hell of a kiss could do that to you."

"I didn't kiss Peter," I say. "I never have."

"Then maybe it's because of his shadow," Jas says. "Tink took it."

"Tink!"

"What?" He lists a little where he's standing, hands trembling by his sides. His face is still distorted, and pale, eyes bruised. "It's not like borrowing a cup of sugar, okay? His shadow really wants me. It's annoying as hell and I didn't invite it over. Well, not expressly."

"Meaning?"

"My magic seems to... suck in shadows," Tink explains. "It's a void. And it's used to Peter's shadow, since he leaves it behind once in a while to go party in the human world."

"What like... like you'd leave a pet in a pet hotel?" I mutter.

"I don't know. Is it?" Tink shrugs. "If so, then it's a hell of a nasty puppy, huh, Peter? How do you live with your shadow? It's one angry motherfucker."

Peter is waking up, thank God, and he blinks at me where I'm bowed over him. "I, uh..." He blinks again, with those long, dark lashes. His eyes are very wide. "I have it under control..."

"Your shadow?" Tink chuckles. "Is that why it's holding onto me right now? That's some impressive mind control... *not*."

"Tink..." I warn.

But Tink is on a roll. "And you lose control around Wendy all the time. You just fucked her. *Again*. You need her like nobody else."

"You fucked her again?" Wes stops struggling in Colt's hold. "Without us?"

"You need her," Tink says again.

"I don't," Peter says, turning his gaze away from me. "That's a fucking lie. You know nothing."

"Hey, guys. I am right here." I glare at Colt and Wes, then at Tink for good measure. "Care to explain to me what's going on? What's the thing with your shadows? Why do they matter so much?"

"Your shadow is your soul," Peter says.

"It's your anchor," Jas says. "Your anchor in the human world. To life. It keeps you from going Fae, from losing substance, from becoming a ghost."

"But you're not ghosts," I protest.

"We all have at least a scrap of shadow. Except for Tink who keeps borrowing Peter's when he isn't here, and now it seems... also when he is."

"Oh, great." Tink rolls his eyes. "Is this going to become a thing, then?" The shadow behind him flares, ebbs and flows. "Shoo, shadow. Go back to the king. Go on!"

Nothing happens.

"Tink lives just fine without a shadow," I say. "So what gives?"

"Fine? Who said he's fine?" Peter snorts. "It's easy for you to say. You have a full shadow. You don't know the madness that lies without."

"Take your shadow back," Tink curses and his sharp teeth flash. "Like she said. I live fine without it."

Peter grimaces. He looks pained, for some reason. Then he closes his eyes, grimacing harder, and Tink lets out a breathy gasp as the shadow wrenches away from him.

He stumbles backward, sitting suddenly down on the ground. "Fuck..."

"There." Peter says, and some color returns to his cheeks. I'm kneeling beside him and I place a hand on his chest to feel him breathing. "All done. Shadow retrieved. Now, Jas, you said you came to tell us something. So spit it out and fuck off."

"Blaming me for what happened here? Real mature." Jas wipes blood from his lips. "Don't apologize too much for beating me up, it makes me uncomfortable."

"Enough lip out of you," I snap, turning to him. "Peter is right. You deserved that, so tell us what you want."

Jas's brows go up. He lifts his hands, too, for good measure. "Don't shoot."

"It's not funny," I mutter.

"You're right, it's not. Peter..." Jas sighs. "You got to listen to me."

Peter's shadow shifts around him, seeping into him. The dullness is leaving his eyes, so yeah, it looks like he needs his shadow, distorted as it is—but then what about Tink? Can he really live without? And how has he done so all this time?

Because he's half-Fae, I was told. But in that case, why—?

"You have to take Wendy back to the human world," Jas says.

Silence greets his words, punctuated only by a soft groan from Tink who's still sitting on his ass, head bowed. I want to go to him, but Peter reaches for me, grabbing my wrist.

"The hell. That's what you came to say?" Peter glares. "That I should take her back?"

"What if I don't want to go back?" I say and suddenly five pairs of eyes are on me. "Not yet, anyway?" I amend. "Not before I figure out how to fix this. How to help you."

"You can't help us," Jas says.

"Says you," Colt mutters.

"Why did you think I sent her back, you idiot?" Hook snaps. "I could have waited for her to die like all the others."

"I don't know," Peter says, "maybe because she's pretty and you're hot for her?"

Jas tsks. "Fuck off."

"Then that leaves only one answer: she's the right one, and you're afraid for her," Wes says.

"God, you're all such fucking idiots," Jas says, "and to think I sacrificed my shadow for you..."

"For us? What a joke." Peter bares his teeth. "How about you make sense for a change? How about you choose a side? First, the Fae brought you here, fuck knows why, and then you were one of us. You swore to save the world and—"

"Save the world?" I glance from Peter's widening eyes to Colt and Wes who look... blank. And Tink, who still looks dazed and out of it. "You said that once but I didn't think you meant it. I thought this was about saving *you*."

"That's what I meant," Peter says, a little too quickly. "Save the island. And us."

"How long will you keep spinning your lies?" Jas says. "She's an adult. An intelligent person. Why don't you explain to her how the worlds are interconnected, how the collapse of one can lead to the—"

"Shut it, Jas," Peter says.

But Jas ignores him. "She's not one of the fragile girls you brought over before. She came back, for fuck's sake. She can take it."

"Hold up," I whisper. "The worlds are connected? Meaning what? I'm... destroying both worlds somehow? That's..." I shake my head. "No, no. Don't put that on me. Having nightmares isn't anything extraordinary. Everyone has them."

"But you're Wendy Darling," Jas says.

"And so what?"

"You come from a long line of powerful women."

"Is that a synonym for witch? I thought we agreed I'm not one." A thought strikes me. "Oh, God, is this a Salem trials nightmare? I did watch a documentary recently on TV..."

Peter has raised himself on one elbow, still gripping my wrist. "It doesn't matter," he says quietly. "None of it matters, except... I wanna know. Why did you take the other side, Jas?"

That's what I want to know, too.

Jas looks bleak. "You know damn well why."

"Enlighten me," Peter says. "I don't know how much time I have."

"Meaning?" It's Jas who asks the question but we're all staring at him now.

Peter rubs a hand over his face. "It's not Wendy who is dying, Jas. It's me."

"No," I whisper.

Jas pales, his face going gray. "Peter."

"It's been too long. My shadow is torn apart, going mad, turning into a beast. I don't have a borrowed one from my buddy the Fae King."

"Fuck you," Jas breathes. "Things have been better since this Wendy came back. I overheard you through the sea, which is closer now. Sometimes I hear your talk. She cured Tink and Wes. She made your memory better."

"It's not enough. I am the fucking island, Jas. I am the Nightmare King."

Oh God... Peter... His fingers are crushing my wrist and I welcome the pain. *No...*

"I know it's not enough," Jas says softly. "Which is why you need to send her back and reset the clock."

"You're not listening to me," Peter grinds out. "I don't care. I can't keep running in this hamster wheel forever. It's not getting better, and at least... at least she's here." Peter tugs on my wrist, pulling me on top of him. "She's *here.*"

"You can't die," Jas says. "You are the center."

"I assure you, I am not." Peter's voice is raw and my heart is cracking open. "I might have been once. King of the nightmare island, the bridge between worlds. The savior the Fae demanded I become."

Under my ear that's pressed to his chest, Peter's heart is racing.

Jas mutters something inaudible, his gaze darkening, then he says, "And where is the center now?"

"Where Wendy is."

"So there is no salvation," Jas says.

"No," Peter replies, and I'm terrified of where this conversation is going.

"Once she faces her fears," Jas says, "the island will sink. She was never meant to save you. Save us."

"No, she wasn't."

"What?" I lift my head but he has wrapped his arm around me, holding me in place. "Peter!"

"But maybe she can sever the link to her world, save it," Jas goes on. "Maybe the Fae will sever it on this side, too. The island, the bridge, will disappear with us on it. You know I'm right. We'll all die."

"So be it," Peter says. "And before it happens, I'll send her back. Because she deserves to live the life we couldn't."

17

WENDY

"Wendy," Peter says, coming after me.

"Don't touch me," I hiss, shrugging his hand off, and keep going, crashing through the trees. "Stay away."

I'm vaguely aware that I should be quieter, more careful, aware the monsters are out there, waiting to attack, but everything that was said is ricocheting inside my head, smashing up my thoughts, overturning the things I thought I had understood.

I mean, that had been pretty screwed up already, but this?

A bridge between worlds, a crumbling bridge that can't be saved, that will take them down with it while Peter wants to send me back...?

But Jas seemed to imply that if I went back now, they might survive...?

"Wendy, wait, dammit!" The voice isn't Peter's but Wes' and I miss a step. "Come back! It's not safe."

I turn around. "According to all I just heard, it's not safe anywhere."

"Wendy..." Tink is standing there, looking pale and drawn,

Wes lending him a shoulder to lean on. "Can we talk about this?"

"I don't want to talk to you," I say. "I want to talk to Jas. Where is he?"

"He left," Colt says.

"You mean, you sent him away."

"No," he says, "I mean he left. He didn't get what he wanted, so why would he stick around?"

"Because this is where he wants to be, with you," I mutter, sad and angry. "If you'd let him."

"So now you're on his side?"

I shrug, angry and hurt. "I don't know."

"You're coming with us," Peter says, coming toward us. "Enough of this."

"I'm not going anywhere with you." I step back but he's fast, advancing on me, grabbing my arm. "Let me go."

Back to the same dance...

"Go where?" he demands. "To the Reds? To the mermaids? I'm not taking you back to your world until you've remembered all there is to remember."

I try in vain to pull my arm free. "But that will destroy the island! It will kill you!"

"Whatever it takes," he says quietly, "to save the worlds, and you."

"I don't want you to put me over everyone else here!" I protest.

"Tough."

"Why are you doing this?"

"Trust me, I don't fucking know why myself." Predictably, he starts dragging me back to camp and I follow, exhausted. "Stop running. I told you from the start."

"I'm not your slave," I bite out. "You can't force me to do things."

He says nothing, and of course he can. They can. Four

muscular men on an island of monsters, with magic at their disposal. What can I do to stop them?

And do I want to? Stop them, that is?

The thought consumes me as we reach the camp—because I don't even know what I want right now, only that I want them to stay alive, stay well, that I don't want anything bad to ever happen to them, which still shocks me when I remember all they've done.

And then the thought fades as all four of them close in, gazing down at me, broad shoulders hemming me in, walling me up at their center.

"You can't talk to Jas," Peter says, using his grip on my arm to yank me against his muscular body. "He's not making any sense."

"And you are?" I breathe, but his scent wraps around me like a spell, lighting up my body, muddying my thoughts.

"You will be okay," Wes says, coming to press his chest to my back, his arms sliding around my waist, under my sweater, under my shirt, warm against my skin. "Trust us."

"We'll protect you," Colt says, closing in on my right side, lifting a strand of my hair to his face, smelling it.

Tink says nothing as he comes against my left side, eyes dark and a little unfocused as he lifts a hand to stroke my cheek.

Then he takes my chin in his hand, turns my head and kisses me.

Kissing Tink is like kissing the night, cool and dark and mysterious, light spice and bitter liquorice root with an aftertaste of honey. I moan as his tongue parts my lips and explores, as it meets mine and swirls, making my blood heat and my body react.

He breaks away way too soon, panting, eyes all black. "No," he whispers.

"Tink."

Backing away, he stops when he fetches against a tree and stays there, eyes still too dark, blinking slowly. His hands ball at his sides.

I try to go after him but the others are on me, tearing at my clothes, mouths twisted into snarls, eyes blazing darkness.

"Guys…" My heart starts to pound for a different reason. "We need to talk some more."

"Fuck first, talk later," Colt growls, "or maybe never. Talking is overrated."

"No, we *have* to talk. I told you, you can't keep changing the topic with sex."

"She's still talking," Wes says. "Someone use that mouth right the hell now."

And even as I fight it, my body wants it, demands it, reacting against my conscious thoughts, arching toward them. I'm bending to their touch like a reed in the wind, trembling as they caress me with their hands, their fingertips, their mouths.

I'm lost at the center of a building storm, a hurricane, not sure which way to turn, who is doing what. I'm sure Colt is the one who has his mouth on my neck, but then Wes claims my mouth, kissing me roughly, while Peter is stroking me—he has ripped my sweater apart, I realize after a while, and my bra, too, and now has his hands on my breasts, squeezing and stroking.

I don't even know who yanks down my pants and panties, leaving me bare, my skin pebbling as a cool breeze blows in from the sea, carrying a whiff of seaweed and fish and rot.

It doesn't matter who.

All I know is the heat of their bodies all around me. I lose sight of Tink as I'm lowered to the ground, on top of someone's shirt.

All their shirts. In between caressing and undressing me, all three apparently took a second to rip off their upper garments and are now kneeling around me in all their bare-chested, muscular glory.

Helplessly, I run my hands over ripped stomachs and tight pecs, over the sexy grooves running into their pants, the fine treasure trails arrowing down, pointing to their crotches and the bulges of erections there.

Oh, sweet Jesus. I feel like I'm about to self-combust. Again, what's wrong with me, getting so aroused in the middle of this mess?

Then again, in my defense, I'm in this mess together with four—no, five, counting Jas—stunning hunks. How am I supposed to keep my cool? If there's a way, I haven't found it yet.

Not used to mind-melts (or melds) caused by studmuffins.

Or any muffins.

Or studs.

See? Can't think straight. Everything is curves and spirals and hot, smooth skin—except for the hard lines of their jaws, their shoulders, their hard cocks tenting their pants.

Dark hair, blond, short, long, skin tattooed or pale or tan, eyes dark or blue or gold—they are like young gods bending over me.

"My turn," Colt says when Peter spreads my legs, reaching a hand between them. "Majesty."

It always jolts me when they address him as king. I keep forgetting that it's how he introduced himself to me.

I still don't understand how he is king and what that means here—king of nightmares, he said, King of Nothing—but Colt doesn't allow me much time to gather my scattered thoughts. His fingers swipe gently between my legs, making me squirm, and then he buries his face there, and I gasp and arch up.

"Colt!" I bury my hands in his long dark hair as he licks and sucks and turns me into a mindlessly rocking, moaning mess. When he uses his tongue to thrust into me, I jerk and moan louder, my insides clenching.

"Enough of that," Peter growls. "She's ready. Let's fuck."

I'd like to say I need more foreplay, always have, that I'm a girl and not a guy who can get hard by inserting a coin into a random slot and can come from the first thrust—but with these guys, I'm always ready, always so hot for them.

Every glance from them, every touch is foreplay where the Lost Boys are concerned.

It's never been that way with any guy. I've never felt so owned, possessed and desired, so willing and ready and desperate to be with someone.

Never felt my body and heart align like this, and it's frigging terrifying, and—

Colt's cock nudges at my entrance and then shoves in without a second warning, filling me up completely, spreading me open. He grabs my arms and hauls me up, into his lap, and I cry out as I sink lower on his thick cock.

With no place to run, I grip his biceps and breathe through it, rocking my hips frantically, practically writhing, until his cock eases all the way in and I'm seated on him, panting, gazing up at his entranced face.

Then Peter presses himself to my back, his very bare cock pressing between my ass cheeks, and beside me Wes is pushing his pants down, freeing a very impressive hard-on that makes my mouth water.

It's sick, feeling so hungry for them, always.

But is it wrong? It doesn't feel wrong, not anymore.

Not when Peter prepares my ass, using my own lubricant and rubbing his cock over my back entrance, smearing it with copious precum, not when he pushes into me while Wes presses the broad head of his cock between my lips.

I'm game. I'm so game for it all, and it makes me so hot and wet I'm ready to come as Colt fucks my pussy while Peter uses my ass and Wes my mouth.

No toys come into play this time—no guns or knives—but Peter slaps my ass as he thrusts, startling a shout out of me, and

Colt plays with my nipples, tugging and twisting while Wes shoves his cock deep until I gag... and start to come.

Unbelievably all of that, the pain and discomfort, it all translates into pleasure and more need, and I swallow around his cock as I come on the hard lengths of the other two, clenching and writhing.

I don't know if they notice my release. They keep fucking me, grunting and breathing unintelligible words that might be my name or curses or God knows what.

Wes starts to come, spilling down my throat, and I swallow convulsively, but it's too much. He pulls out before I choke and sprays the rest all over my breasts, striping them in white, groaning.

"Oh fuck..." Colt's cock twitches inside my pussy, swelling impossibly bigger, making me gasp and bend lower over him—and he sucks one of my nipples into his mouth.

I cry out at the sensation that leads straight to my core, and where I was still shuddering with the aftershocks of my orgasm, now I'm tightening again, my entire body trembling as the two boys fuck me hard, harder than before.

Holding onto my hips, Colt lifts and lowers me on his cock while thrusting up, his jaw tight, his eyes shut, while Peter is pounding my ass like a possessed man.

"You're not leaving," he grunts with every thrust. "Not leaving. No leaving... *fuck.*"

I'm about to come again, and it's going to be huge, an earth-shattering, mind-blowing, body-crashing orgasm that's starting deep inside of me, deeper than ever before—and where I'm bent over Colt, my hands braced on either side of his head as he sucks on my nipple, as Peter pounds into me—I see Tink.

He's watching us, leaning back against a tree trunk. He has his cock out and jacking off desperately, his face red, his breathing chopped.

I whisper his name, reach out a hand for him, needing him

to join us, but he hisses and starts to come in great spurts all over his chest, over his T-shirt, his cum hitting his chin, and it's so coarse and erotic I cry out, convulsing as I come again, the pleasure too much to contain, too much to comprehend.

I could almost die of pleasure right now, so lost in it I'd let the island sink with all of us on it...

18

WES

Coming in her mouth is a mind-fuck –it feels so damn good that I'm reeling, but still all I want is to shove Colt aside, get between her legs and sink inside her.

Sharing her with the others, though, that's damn hot. I'm still hard, after coming so violently I almost fell over, and then I see Tink jacking off and coming all over himself, sliding down the trunk, and fuck...

That's hot, too.

I feel a kinship with Tink, and not only because Wendy somehow brought us back from the brink of death together.

There's always been something vulnerable and fragile in Tink, buried under layers of aggression and spiky defiance that reminds me of myself when I first arrived on the island.

Not that Tink is weak. Never in a million years. He's one of the strongest people I know, brave and gallant. A constant friend. A damn crazy bastard.

But he's hiding a wound deep like the sea that's still bleeding and he won't let anyone help him.

Nowadays, I have Colt at my back, helping me up whenever

the demons of the past get too strong and drag me down. And Tink has Peter, I guess, but Peter is an insane sadist.

That must be what they call 'the blind leading the blind,' right? How can Peter help him when Peter has spent the past few centuries barely remembering his own name and barely caring about anything beyond himself and his mission?

Tink was his soldier, his bodyguard, his only friend until we arrived—that was long after the fallout with Jas—and although Peter cares about him, Peter isn't in a position to help him.

And maybe it's stupid to worry about Tink when our world is about to end—our fight, our lives—but I can't help it.

Tucking my dick in my pants, I go to him and reach a hand down. "Tink."

He ignores my hand, grabbing at the tree trunk to get up. "What the fuck," he hisses. "What's going on with you?"

I frown. "But it's—"

"I'm talking to Peter," Tink says, lifting his head, his green gaze spitting flames. His face is pale, feverish spots on his cheeks and I wonder if the poison still runs in his veins after all. "Our infatuated king."

"Now, just a sec," Peter says, still entangled with Wendy whose naked curves make me swallow hard, my dick twitching with renewed interest. "What's your problem, Tink?"

"My problem?" Tink lets out an incredulous snort. "My problem is you making plans without consulting us, making decisions—"

"I'm your fucking king!" Peter bites out. "This isn't a democracy."

"But we are your..." Tink stops, paling more. He turns to me as if looking for support but I don't know what he's driving at. "He hasn't even cut her with his knives. Blood fascinates him. Now he's more fascinated by *her*."

"Why?" Wendy asks, sitting back and though a small moan escapes her—because she's still connected to Peter and Colt, obviously—she manages to go on, "Why is he fascinated by blood?"

Tink sighs. "Because he killed his abusive uncle when he was young—"

"Shut up, Tinker," Peter snaps. "I don't wanna talk about that."

"Oh, I see. Am I the only one who has to face her fears?" she mutters, turning her face, trying to see Peter over her shoulder.

"It's not fear," Peter says. "It's a fact. An act done long ago, one I don't wish to discuss—"

"—with the present company?" She starts lifting herself off them, and Peter wraps his arms around her middle, keeping her down.

"It was too long ago," he says.

"But it still haunts you," she argues.

"She's got a point there," Tink says.

Peter snarls. "Oh, fuck off. Don't listen to him, Wendy."

"Now you remember her name," Tink says. "And you don't need my help, obviously, now that your memory is better. Did you stop cutting yourself, too?"

"Dammit, shut the hell up!" Peter roars, and a cold wind blows. Dark clouds are gathering and lightning splits the sky.

"You're changing Peter's shadow," I tell Tink. "Maybe that's why he's remembering."

"Oh? It's not the magical sex with her?" Tink tucks himself in, too, runs his hands over his dirty clothes. "Think his friends might have something to do with it? You must be wrong, Wes. The new girl is all he really needs."

"Goddammit, Tink!" Now Peter is the one trying to get up, but Tink only gives him the finger and stalks off. "My memory is better because she came back! That's why and you know it. But maybe you're right, maybe it has to do with you, too, I... Wait!"

I don't need Peter to tell me to go after him. With a last glance at Colt and Wendy and my King, I leave the clearing.

————

"Tink!" I yell. "Wait, man, just… wait. Fuck!"

He's quick like lightning, darting through the woods, more fox or cat than human, his Fae nature showing more than ever in his light tread and the way he blends in with nature. A flash of pink, a flash of gold and copper, the sharp tang of magic on the air, that's his trail.

"Tink, son of a bitch! Come back here!" I run through the woods, chasing the flashes, the magic, the impressions of a young boy running and laughing, followed by glimpses of a winged man weeping, reaching for me. "Stop the magic, damn you!"

Suddenly, he's right in front of me, head bowed, fists clenched at his sides, sharp teeth bared, and I skid to a halt, almost sliding to the ground.

"Jesus," I pant.

"Not a name I go by," he growls.

"Come on, Tink, relax—"

He grabs me by the neck with one hand and lifts me in the air, his mouth stretched too wide, his eyes burning like coals, his hair turning into writhing snakes and flowering twigs.

"Tink. Stop. Dammit." I'm choking but trying to pry his hand off my windpipe seems to be having no effect. Sharp nails are cutting into my flesh, burning points around the crushing pressure and pain and the hand stopping my airflow. "Tink!"

Something shifts in his face, so unfamiliar in its grotesque Fae distortion, a flicker of uncertainty in his all-black-and-red eyes.

His hand opens.

I crumple to the ground, coughing.

Fuck.

He takes a step back, then another. In my blurry vision, I think I see panic on his face, but then he turns away. "Fuck off," he says. "Go back to daddy."

I almost laugh through the hacking. "You talk of friends and look how you treat them."

"I'm not..." He curses, jaw clenching. "I needed a minute."

"Time doesn't matter, Tink." I cough, my throat raw. "Not if you don't use it."

"What the fuck is that supposed to mean?"

"You know exactly what it means." Slowly I get to my feet, still wheezing. I rub at my aching neck. "And you can't even look me in the eye."

His shoulders rise and fall on a breath. "What do you want to hear? That I'm sorry? You'll live."

"You're an asshole."

"And you're too human to understand me. Or are you the changeling, after all?" He snorts, turns to face me—same old Tink, pretty and bright, all colors and pleasing shapes. "Tell me, since we're talking about trust."

"Are we? Talking about trust?" I wipe at my mouth. "Because you don't trust me."

"No further than I can throw you," he agrees.

"I'm heavy."

"Pure muscle." He nods. "All of you, guys. I've noticed."

"You're not too bad yourself."

A muscle ticks in his jaw. He chews on the inside of his cheek. "What do you want from me, Wes?"

So much. I've wanted so much from Tink, from all of us, but it somehow never happened, never seemed possible, until...

Until Wendy Darling appeared.

I can't explain all that, can't express it, especially when he acts so guarded and wary, claws and fangs coming out whenever I try to get close—and yet I can't help myself. Like with Wendy, I find myself drawn to Tink more than the others.

His pain calls to me.

So I take a step closer, and another, convinced he's going to turn and run once more as I reach for him.

He doesn't move, still as a statue, watching my approach through slitted eyes. His hands unclench at his sides. So calm to all appearances, but a vein is beating fast in his neck, betraying him.

"You keep running," I say, standing nose to nose with him, falling into the green of his eyes, green like a forest, green like grass, like tropical lagoons and shallow seas. "Why? What are you afraid of? That I'll make you feel things? That your body might decide it wants me, wants us? That your heart might agree?"

"Step away," he growls but makes no move himself. "Wes…"

I lift a hand, grip his jaw. "Tell me you don't want me, *us*, that you feel nothing for us, that you don't give a shit, that you don't feel a lick of desire, and I'll go back to camp and leave you to cool down on your own. Just tell me."

"Don't," he says, still not moving, though his chest is rising and falling faster now. "Don't, Wes."

"Why, what will happen if I keep touching you, if I stay, if I kiss you—"

"By all the ancient gods," he growls, baring those strangely sexy sharp teeth again, "what do you want from me?"

"To tell me what the problem is, you went off like that at Peter. It wasn't the first time, either. Are you…" I risk it. "Are you jealous of Wendy?"

"So any anger I might harbor would be due to a petty lovers' spat?" he asks, his voice tight.

"You're not Peter's lover." I pause, watching his face. "You're nobody's lover."

He waves a hand. "Details."

"Are they just details, though?"

"You don't get it," he whispers.

"Then *help* me get it."

"Does it fucking matter?" he spits the words out one by one. "The end is coming, one way or another, and I can't stop it. Nobody can. I had hoped for a long time that Wendy would save us, and then... then I'd let myself feel and be who I want to be, but as it turns out, hope was a traitor and even this Wendy can't help us. The island will go down in the waves and Wendy will go back to the human world and that's it, Wes. That's *it*. That's all, that's the *end*."

"You don't know that," I breathe.

"Our king has decided. Who are we to gainsay him?"

"But—"

"And he's probably right," Tink says. "I don't see any other way to fulfill our mission. I just wish..."

"What?"

He clenches one hand into a fist, raises it. "That we ever had a chance. Turns out we were born without it. And yet..."

"Talk to me."

"Nothing to say." Dismissive. Hard. "Go back."

"Not without you," I tell him. "Not before we talk."

"Talk about what?" he snarls. "Sex? Desire? You think I don't want you? Think I can't get hard? That I'm incapable of getting aroused?"

"No, I..."

I saw you earlier, I want to tell him, *I saw how hard you were, how hard you came*—but suddenly he's caging me against the tree and a very hard erection is rubbing against my hip. Those deep green eyes are blazing into my eyes and then they drop to my mouth.

He kisses me. Pressing his lips to mine, imprinting the shape of his mouth on mine, his tongue thrusting against my tongue. He slants his head to deepen the kiss more and I groan helplessly, so hard I think I'm gonna bust.

I lift my hands to cup his face, map it, Christ, *finally*, to slide my thumbs over the straight line of his jaw, to cradle his head—and he tears himself off me, shoving at my chest.

"Fuck." His eyes are wild, too wide and kind of blank. "Hell, what am I...?" And turning, he starts back toward the camp.

Leaving me rattled and wanting and damn hard and—

"Tink, wait, dammit." I jog after him. "*Wait.*"

"No, I can't. Fucking can't," he's muttering as if to himself, "not even when I had Peter's shadow, I... It didn't work. I thought maybe with a girl, I could but... Girls aren't any better, dammit."

"Tink." I grab his arm to slow him down but he twists and slaps my hand off him. "Did your father... did he... did he hurt you? I just—"

"My father?" He stops at the edge of the clearing where the others have finally extricated themselves and are pulling on clothes, throws his head back and laughs.

I'm fucking confused. "What's so damn funny?"

"*Her* father hurt her, perhaps." He points at Wendy. "I never knew mine, though he was an asshole alright."

"But then...?"

"You lack imagination. It's not like I grew up in a dungeon. Plenty of guys and girls in the world."

"Tink..."

"My father was a *korrigan* king, but nasty as he is, he was never a part of my life. Big fat load of good that did me in the end," Tink says bitterly. "My mother left me for the freak I was, and after that, it all went downhill."

"That much I can imagine," I mutter. "Not like the rest of us had it easy, man."

He nods, acknowledging that. He knows my history, and Colt's.

"Then who abused you, Tink? Who made you afraid of touching, of letting go?"

"Too damn many people," he says darkly and bends to grab an apple from the pile, ignoring the rest of us. "And I think we've talked enough."

19

WENDY

"Tink, Wes, where were you?" I've put on a dress from the trunk, and God, I'd give anything for a hot shower right now, but the thought of washing in the sea with the freaky mermaids is... a no-no. "It's dangerous to wander off like that."

Tink snorts, bites into the apple in his hand. Magic sparks and fizzles around him, his hair dark and lifting with electricity. "*Dangerous*." He speaks the word like it's a joke.

"Yes, with the Reds—"

"Mmm." He chews thoughtfully. "Why don't you guys keep fucking, to keep your minds off reality? You were doing so well until now."

My heart starts to pound. "Am I supposed to be embarrassed? Because, you know, Tink, I won't let you make me feel that way. We're adults here. We wanted it. Sorry you don't want to take part."

"Yeah, well, I've had enough of bread and circuses, thank you."

"Oh, come off it, Tinker," Colt snaps. "Stop acting like you're better than the rest of us."

"Better?" He appears to think about it. "No. Cleverer? Oh, yeah."

"Yeah? Is avoiding pleasure some secret weapon we don't know about? Something the monks told you, perhaps? Because…" Colt stretches muscular arms over his head. "It feels good. Sure you don't wanna try?"

"Are you offering her?" Tink nods at me, still chewing. "For my use?"

"Hey, now," I mutter. "No need to be nasty."

"But it's what I do best." He turns his back to us, kicks at a pebble. Spits out an apple seed. "It's who I am. A nasty mongrel."

"No, Tink. It's not." Peter has pulled on a pair of black pants he found in the trunk and a clean white old-fashioned shirt, still unbuttoned. The whirls of ink on his skin seem to writhe. The old scar on his chest is an angry, deep purple. His shadow wavers behind him, snapping away as if trying to escape.

Trying to reach Tink who's chewing on his bite of the apple, gaze distant.

While Colt and Wes gaze at each other, as if communicating without words, their common shadow hovering between them like a fraying dark ghost.

"You gave up," Tink says, spitting out another seed, this time in Peter's direction. "Some king you are. You were supposed to fix the island, fix the bridge, fix the nightmares. Not let it sink."

"Oh, so now you have problems with my leadership?"

More chewing. "Shocker, right?"

"Not really. Everyone's a critic."

"But not everyone is a king." Tink arches a copper brow. "Maybe it's time to abdicate?"

Peter bares his teeth. "Why, want the crown?"

"Is that what that nest on your head is?"

"Fuck you, Tink. You know I didn't want the throne."

"How sad, yeah, I know." Tink nods. "Poor little king, forced to rule. Did you ever ask yourself why they chose you? Why this island needed a king at all?"

"Your point being?"

I want to ask the same, to stop this argument, this fight between them.

"That you have been a fucking little pawn in their game?" Tink says. "That they set you up to fail all along? You tell us, Peter, why you? Why a human?"

"I don't fucking know!" Peter yells.

"Really?" This time Tink throws the apple core at Peter. It thumps against his bare, inked chest and falls to the ground. "Want us to believe that?"

"Tink," Wes says, a note of warning in his voice that Tink ignores.

"You say you killed one of the Fae—how, when?" Tink wanders closer to Peter, an arrogant swagger. "How did you end up here, you and Jas? What's the real story?"

Peter is staring at him. "Goddammit, what's the matter with you these days?"

"As opposed to the centuries past? I dunno, Peter, you tell me." Tink lifts his chin, jaw clenched. "Maybe I got too old for you?"

Peter gapes. He looks like he's keeping himself from grabbing Tink and shaking him by sheer force of will. "What's *that* supposed to mean?"

"It means... Damn, forget it."

"*Forget* it? You think you can just throw accusations in my face and then storm off every time?" Peter's shadow expands and shrinks, then expands again, a pulsing thundercloud. I start when I realize a skull is showing underneath Peter's face. His dark hair whips about his face although there's no wind. "I thought you knew me better than this. You, of all people. On whose side are *you* on, anyway, Tink?"

"I dunno anymore." Tink's eyes narrow. "Maybe I'll go find Jas. Maybe he's onto something."

Peter roars, the black ink on his skin writhing, lifting off into spikes and blades, his shadow swelling and rising like a hurricane, pulling in leaves and twigs, whipping over him.

It dives at Tink who curses and throws flames and sparks at it, his magic twisting around him like armor.

"Peter! Stop this!" I rush to him and grab his arm, but I cry out when power slams into me, sending me to the ground, on my ass. I blink up at the sky and the swirling clouds.

Whoa.

"Wendy. Wendy, are you all right?" Three faces are bent over me. The hurricane, the magic, the shadows are dissipating. I don't ask myself anymore if I imagined it all. I just blink, waiting for my vision to clear, and slowly sit up.

Peter crouches down grabs my wrist and... I let him pull me against his chest. Strangely, it feels safe.

"Are you all right?" I whisper. "Is Tink okay? Where is he?"

Tink comes to stand over me. "Take your goddamn shadow back, Peter. I told you so many times, I don't want it. I don't want you to share it with me."

"You need it, asshole," Peter snaps.

"Is that what you have been doing?" I whisper, turning to Peter. "Sharing your shadow with him?"

"He'll die without a shadow," Peter says, his voice a low rumble. "He's half-human."

"Newsflash," Tink says. "We're all going to die for this noble cause, Wendy excepted, so stop trying to force life into me, all right?"

"The Twins share their shadow. Why can't we?"

"Fuck your shadow. It's a mess anyway. Needs a wash and a mend."

Peter barks a laugh. It shakes his body, shakes me. "Dammit."

But the reality I'd tried to ignore, just like Tink had accused us of doing, comes crashing back down on me.

"We're all going to die for this noble cause."

I can't let this happen. Assholes or not, virtual strangers who have somehow managed to snag my heart, I'm not letting them die if there is another way.

I push away from Peter, slowly climb to my feet. He rises with me, his shadow detaching from Tink and sliding back into him.

"You sure you're all right?" Colt asks, those dark eyes seeing right through me. "What's on your mind?"

"Nothing," I lie.

"Bullshit," Wes says. "Since Jas came here, talking out of his ass, you've been lost in thought."

"And in sex," Tink mutters.

"Was he, though? Talking out of his ass?" I glance at their serious faces. "You admitted he was right. You can't keep the truth from me anymore. I'm going to talk to Jas."

"No way," Colt says.

"Wendy," Peter says, "no."

"I have to find a solution," I protest. "I can't let you die! You can't ask this of me."

"But the worlds—"

"I don't frigging care!" I'm breathing hard, my chest too tight. "There has to be another way. I'm not going to sink the island, sink you—"

"You can't leave," Wes whispers. "Can't leave us, Wendy."

I don't want to leave them, that's the problem. or rather, that's not the problem—the problem is that if I stay, I'll kill them with my nightmares. I don't know how this makes any sense, but that's what I understood.

God, I need to speak to Jas and...

"Peter is right," Wes says, "you can't leave, not before you've faced your past."

I lift my chin, meet his gaze. "And destroyed the island in doing so?"

"If that's what it takes. Look, what if we thought there was a way to survive this? We swore to save the worlds. That's what matters the most."

"I don't care!" I tell him. "I can't let you die."

"You don't know us," Colt says. "Maybe we deserve to die."

I shake my head. "No."

"You said you have brothers," Colt continues. "You will go back to them. Your world safe. Your family intact. It's the least. The least you can do for us."

God...

They shouldn't. They shouldn't care about me or the worlds. They should care about themselves, about making it through this mess.

Did they suddenly grow a heart beneath the violent, spiky exteriors, or is it a misguided sense of responsibility for the universe that guides them? Whatever it is, it looks like they're on a path of self-destruction to save the rest of us.

Jas was right. For the first time, I understand what he's been fighting for, and I'm on his side. This can't happen. I can't let the Lost Boys go down with the ship.

"I need to find him," I say, "now."

"You're not going to Jas," Peter says, reaching for me again, "Wendy—"

I shove at him—not with my hands but with my whole body, a wave of *something* leaving me, a force that slams into the four of them and sends them down on their asses—like before, with the trees, like—

Don't remember, don't think, don't go under.

I turn around and run.

———

I RUN ONCE MORE AMONG THE TREES BUT THIS TIME NOBODY follows me, no running footsteps, no voices. After a while, I slow down, trying to catch my breath.

How come they didn't come after me? Did I really knock them out? Worry starts worming its way into my heart. I turn around, look back in the direction from which I came.

The woods close in around me, darkening, trails narrowing, confining, eyes blinking from every corner.

Oh shit. Fear shoots through me. What have I done?

"Jas!" I call out, turning in a circle. "Hook! Can you hear me? Where are you?"

As if he'd lurk around, waiting for me to show up.

Okay, Dee, deep breaths.

I take a few steps, as quietly as I can, tiptoeing on the faint trail, my steps crunching too loudly on dead leaves and litter.

I shouldn't have run away like that, but sitting on my ass and doing nothing—well, apart from having sex with them, so much sex, and God was that *hot*, and the wetness running down my legs reminds me of every little detail, and if I self-combust, will that count as evading the Reds?—yeah, doing nothing isn't okay.

I cling to that belief as I start again to run, glancing over my shoulder the entire time, stumbling over fallen branches and hollows, my heart banging hard enough to break a rib. I think I hear noises in the woods, crashes and rumbles, I think I see red flashes.

The Reds.

They found me.

They're coming for me.

Racing faster, I shove away low-hanging branches that keep slapping me in the face, one of them scratching my cheek. The slight burn of the small wound distracts me. I glance over my shoulder once more—and run smack into something solid, my head thumping against it.

Arms windmilling, I fall, and I scream when something clamps on my arm, almost wrenching it out of its socket, stopping my fall. I hang there, all but dangling from that hold.

"Well, well," a low male voice says and a smug smile fills my vision. A ticking sound fills the air. "Wendy Darling. What's up with all of you guys, stomping through the woods without any concern for your wellbeing? Do you all want to die?"

Hook.

Jas.

He's right in front of me, holding me up by my arm, a bemused look in his gray eyes. His white shirt is spattered with blood, his old-fashioned gray pants are creased and grimy.

In his other hand, he's holding a crocodile-skin pocket watch, as if he's been checking the hour, measuring time.

His shadow warriors stand behind him, a dark crowd.

"There you are," I breathe, injecting as much nonchalance as I can into my voice, forcing my buckling knees to straighten, pulling my arm away. "I was looking for you."

"Now *that*," he says, dropping his pocket watch back into his pants pocket, his smirk widening into a grin, "is a goddamn twist, if I ever saw one."

20

JAS

"And yet I don't know what we have to talk about," I tell her, raking my eyes over her pretty face, her sexy body in that red dress. "I sent you back to your world. You returned right here."

"I did." Fuck, her voice is sweet. "This is your camp?"

"Indeed."

She glances around, blond hair sticking to her sweaty face, her rosy cheeks glowing. "Where is everyone?"

I lick my lips, feeling like the wolf who just met Red Riding Hood and decided to eat her up. "Who did you expect?"

"I don't know... people. Your army."

"You've seen my army." I gesture at the shadows gathering around the clearing. "There it is."

"But..."

I take a deep breath and a growl rumbles up in my chest. "Damn, you smell so good. I fucking can't..." I rub a hand over my face, then over my chest, because it doesn't just hit me in the balls, it hits me everywhere. It makes me antsy. "What do you want here, Wendy?"

"I want you to send me back," she whispers. "Back to the human world."

"Oh, just that?" I try to control my breathing. "You think it's that easy, sending someone across the Veil? Do you think perhaps that it's something I do every day before breakfast?"

"Perhaps?" she says. "Flexing your magical muscles before eating is a good idea. Builds appetite."

I give an incredulous laugh. "Are you for real?"

"How should I know? This is all nuts." She nods at my Pirates, her small face tightening. "Why are they staring at me? It's creepy."

"The shadows? They aren't staring at you." I wave a dismissive hand.

"They are turned my way."

"They are at rest," I explain. "I don't require them right this moment."

She squints at them with mistrust. "You already have a shadow. So what are they?"

"Shadows without a body. Shades. Ghosts."

"Ghosts..." She seems to be turning the word over in her mouth, in her mind. "All of them? All are ghosts? Without a corporeal body?"

"That's right. They aren't great conversationalists, either, I have to tell you."

"This... isn't funny," she whispers.

"Damn right it isn't."

It's taking her quite some time to figure it out but she's been hit by shock after shock, so it doesn't surprise me.

What surprises me is the sharpness in her voice when she says, "Are you telling me that you live here with ghosts as your only company?"

Ah, the penny has dropped. "Well, yeah—"

"So you live, in fact, all alone?"

I open my mouth to retort something, make light of it, crack some stupid sarcastic joke, but... nothing comes out. Because she's hit the nail on the head and straight into my chest, stopping my breath.

Stopping my goddamn heart.

"You must be lonely," she says.

Oh, yeah. You could say that.

Dying of loneliness.

All alone with the ghosts, nobody to speak to, nobody to touch, to share a moment with, to share my fears and worries, to share the tiny joys of finding a good knife I can use in the woods, of getting a clean change of clothes from my keepers.

Of knowing the Lost Boys are still alive.

No partner. No friends.

Not anymore.

But I don't say all that. I never do, but my hands betray me, pulling out my pocket watch to check the time.

"Why do you do that?" she whispers. "What importance would time have here, the passing minutes and hours?"

"I don't count minutes or hours," I mutter. "I count years and decades and centuries. It's a countdown to the end of time, to the Night of Nights."

She gazes at me, her blue eyes deep like the sea. "The mermaids gave it to you."

I close my hand around the watch. Grind my teeth. "Alliances had to be forged. I made my choice and have my mission."

"To get the crown."

"To save the Lost Boys." I swallow a sigh. "You don't believe me, either."

"If I didn't, I wouldn't have looked for you. I meant, get the crown and so save them from themselves."

She believes me. She's digging claws into my heart, no, not claws. Feathers. Softness and gentleness, and that's the only way to break me.

"You know what?" I gesture at her. "Why don't you tell me why you really came to see me."

"Excuse me?"

"Are you really that worried over a few guys you barely know? Or did you just wanna see *me*?"

"I..." Her gaze moves over my face, lingers on my mouth. "I don't..."

Unsure, but interested. Caught off guard.

All right.

When I step closer and reach for her, she comes willingly.

Yeah, baby. I can work with that. I know that isn't why she came, but I can't help her and can't have her feeling any fucking pity for me, no. I couldn't stand that.

Much better to divert the conversation, or rather, end it. I may be doomed and dead inside but I'm still horny, and she turns me on like no girl ever has.

It's not just her scent, roses and toffee and candies, making my mouth water and my dick hard, but everything about her. She touches parts of my soul I thought had withered and died.

Oh, *fuck* that. Won't dwell on that. Can't afford to.

She was never mine to start with, and now Peter and the Lost Boys have claimed her and decided to save her, so what's left for me to do here? I'd say my job is done, but I'm the one who's done. My usefulness ended. The reasons for my existence, for my war, annihilated.

Redundant, superfluous. Undesired.

Nothing new there, huh, Jas? You made your choices, had other choices made for you, and accepted your fate.

Loneliness, she calls it. *Yeah*. That's a tame word for the savagery of it. The brutal isolation of it.

But she desires me right now, and I'll take what I can, before it's all over.

———

Kissing her feels like plunging into cool water, but at the same time, her sweetness fills me up, flows into every part of me. It has to be a law of physics, something about opposites attracting that pulls us together like this, my bitter, broken parts seeking her soft, delicious curves.

We shouldn't fit together, and yet we fit perfectly as I haul her against me.

She gasps and I groan, and we kiss harder. A thrill grips me when her tongue touches mine, when she winds her arms around my neck, her breasts pressing into my chest, so full and round and fucking sexy, her nipples hard, her body hot and supple, molding to mine.

God damn. Fucking hell, she feels good.

Too good.

And this foreign shadow I have riding my ass wants her, too, though it wants different things from her—violent, painful things, things that try to intrude into my thoughts.

Hell, what am I saying? They keep intruding, day in and day out, and right now they fill my head with images of everything I could do to her, ways to hurt her as I pleasure her.

Dark thoughts.

I splay my hand over her ass, grabbing it hard, while with the other I grab a fistful of her hair and yank her head back, still kissing her. I want to bite her, bind her, spread her, lash her, use her…

It's hard to stop it, to stop the shadow, to stop my own raw need for her. My scar aches dully. I'm pretty sure Peter got my heart when he stabbed me that time long ago, but I'm not supposed to have a heart, am I? I'm a creature of need.

I'm made of it.

Unlike the Lost Boys, I didn't have Peter to bring back girls from time to time, girls to touch and kiss and fuck. Wendies. I've been more celibate than a monk on this island, focused on my mission, spending my nights in the company of my right hand.

Instead, I have this asshole shadow who wants to fuck her up instead of just fuck her.

She squirms against me and my shadow snarls and latches on to her. My tongue thrusts deep inside her mouth, tasting all that sweetness, all her struggle, my hands tightening on her, surely leaving bruises—and... she just relaxes against me once more, her hands locking behind my head.

As if she wants that.

Needs that.

Giving up on trying to control my shadow or myself, I break the kiss, pick her up and slam her to the ground, on her back, startling a cry out of her.

Fuck, she looks so hot like this, her hair spreading in a golden lake around her, her eyes wide, mouth reddened and cheeks pink, her breasts rising and falling with every rapid breath, straining the thin fabric of the red dress she put on.

"I hope you don't like this dress too much," I growl—my shadow pulsing with excitement as I grab the cleavage and pull, tearing it open, letting her titties spill out.

She gasps, tries to sit up, but I'm on top of her, shredding the dress from top to bottom, parting the fabric, leaving her bare.

No panties, no bra.

Perfect.

"Jas," she says, her cheeks crimson, "I—"

"Shush." I grip her chin, turn her head to the side, speak into the delicate shell of her ear. "You're going to spread for me, give me what I want. I bet you're so fucking wet already. Wet for me, aren't you, little slut of the Lost Boys?"

She gasps. "But—"

"You'll take it. Because you like it rough, hard and fast. Because you like me forcing you to fucking take it, taking away your options. Your responsibility. You like me using you for my own fucking pleasure."

I don't expect a reply but a soft "yes" escapes her as she arches up a little, the flush spreading down her neck to her tits.

God fucking dammit.

It's as if she understands my shadow, my demon, and wants it, too. My shadow fucking *purrs* at the sound of her submission.

No wonder Peter and the Boys went crazy about her. No wonder my head is such a mess, my thoughts all over the place, my goddamn body burning for her.

My shadow wants me to hurt her, torment her. My need for her consumes me. The need to own her, control her, eats at me.

"You shouldn't have come here, girl," I tell her softly, releasing her chin. "Don't you know I'm the worst of them? Didn't they tell you? Haven't you fucking noticed that I am the enemy?"

"I told you, I don't believe it," she whispers, eyes wide.

"This place is built of nightmares, but I *am* the nightmare. I don't have a soul. This shadow isn't mine."

"Whose is it?" she breathes. "I thought it was a Fae shadow."

"A dead man's soul. Fae or human, what does it matter?" I pull out my belt, feel it slither through the loops around my hips, then grab her wrists, lift them over her head, press them to the ground. "It wants you. I want you." I lean in, leer at her. "So ready or not, here I come."

She struggles a little, panic flashing over her face, behind the mirrors of her blue eyes, when I lift my belt. "Jas..."

"Don't make me use the belt in different ways. Trust me, my shadow wants me to. I'd hate to leave welts on that fine skin of yours." Okay, that's a lie, I'd love that, but fighting my shadow has become second nature, and I stop it before going further.

Too far.

Far enough.

I gaze down at her curves, so soft and inviting. So damn hot. I run the leather belt over her tits, her neck, her lips, pass the buckle over her cheeks, and she whimpers. Her lips form my name.

I grin down at her. "This won't hurt... much."

Her eyes widen more, but before she can say anything, I flip her on her stomach, pushing her face down into the soft soil, then I bind her hands together with my belt, behind her back.

She squirms, and it's hard to make out words since she's eating dirt but I think she's cursing.

I shouldn't be grinning so fucking wide, shouldn't be feeling so elated. I wasn't always like this. But my shadow is full of glee and pride and horniness, it's goddamn aroused, and so am I.

And I mount her, like an animal, pushing down my fly and pulling out my aching cock, shoving it into her wet pussy, thrusting deep. She wails, tries to shake me off, but I push her down and start to rock.

"Jas..." She's still squirming.

"Stay still." Lifting my hand, I slap her ass, hard, and she gasps. Squirms some more.

Down comes my hand again, leaving a red imprint on her pale flesh. I love how it looks. A mark. A brand.

Mine.

Her breath comes out shaky. A sob escapes her.

So I do it again.

And again.

While using her pussy. Hot, tight, soaked, perfect. The sounds of my cock slamming into her again and again are music to my ears. My shadow roars its approval. The watching ghosts titter and clap.

I'm about to come. Not sure if she is, too. Doesn't matter. She came to me. So she is mine. I want to put a collar on her. Tie her up. Keep her here.

And to hell with the world.

21

WENDY

The old-fashioned, handsome gentleman I met the previous times—the one who spoke gently to me and sent me back to my world, the one who saved the Lost Boys time and again—is gone. In his place is a beast, snarling and roaring, hurting me and using me.

I saw it before he flipped me on my belly: the dark, alien shadow with the branching horns, like an old god of the forest. A lusty, violent god that has possessed Jas, turning his gray eyes a pupil-less black, his mouth into a rictus.

A dead man's ghost, he said, but it feels like something more twisted and dark.

And yet my body betrays me, *liking* it. It frigging likes the way he uses me, the way he takes away my options and makes me take it—the sting of pain from his slaps, from the belt biting into my wrists, the uncomfortable position, his big cock ramming into me.

I'm eating dirt and dry leaves, my bare breasts dragging against the soil and sharp pebbles, my nipples aching. My ass is in the air, burning from his slaps, my pussy burning from the savage invasion of his cock.

And I'm writhing in pleasure, about to come, my belly tightening, my ass cheeks clenching, the orgasm starting deep inside of me, making me gasp, then cry out as I try to rock back, on his hard cock.

He grips my hip and stops me.

It doesn't matter. I'm coming, cries leaving my lips as I clench again and again, my release rocking me like an explosion.

He curses, hunching over my back, his cock jerking inside me, spilling heat. His grip on my hip hurts, but the pain is washed away in the flood of pleasure still rushing through me.

I love the heat of his muscular body over me, the feel of his still-hard cock lodged inside me, and I whimper as aftershocks pulse through me. Not sure how much pleasure my body can contain before it breaks apart, cracking down the middle like the clay vessel it is.

We're both panting. My body is slick with sweat. He pulls out of me and the musky scent of his cum is everywhere. It's already dripping down my thighs.

It feels like my arms are about to be wrenched out of their sockets. "Jas..."

He doesn't untie me. Doesn't move for a long moment.

Then he grabs my tied-up hands and drags me backward through the dirt. I yell at him to stop. It really hurts. But he doesn't seem to hear me. He's snarling words I can't make out under his breath.

Good God. He's as crazy as Peter, his mind split, torn between himself and his feral shadow.

He leaves me against the tree trunk, bared and scratched all over, leaking semen and tears I can't hold back—not so much from pain or fear as from that violent release and the confusion accompanying it.

Somewhere in the back of my mind is the thought that I came here to talk to him, not to have sex, not to be roughened up and tied up by a man who is barely human anymore.

"Jas," I try again, wondering how and when I can get through to him. He's standing there, hands fists at his sides, big shoulders hunched, his half-hard cock still jutting out of his pants. "Jas! Hey!"

He turns his back to me and stalks away. His ghost soldiers turn with him, trotting after him.

"Hey! You can't just leave me here!" This is like a déjà vu. "Untie me! Jas!"

He takes a few more steps and stops. Tilts his head to the side as if listening to something. "Fuck," he growls.

"Jas!"

His head twitches toward me. His ghosts twitch with him. "Wendy?"

"Untie me! I came to talk."

He growls something more and turns back around, tucking himself inside his pants, zipping up. He runs a hand through his silver-blond hair, only succeeding in ruffling it more, raising it into funny spikes. "What happened?"

"You just fucked me!" I seethe. "Don't tell me you already forgot all about me. I'd believe it of Peter, not you."

"No, I..." He blinks. Comes to finally untie me, his expression dark. "It's just this shadow... it was talking to me."

"Talking? About what?"

"The ways... the ways I can use you. Hurt you."

"God... You and Peter... you are so similar in many ways," I mutter as he crouches down and unwraps the leather belt from around my chafed wrists. I rub at them.

"You mean in the monstrous ways our shadows control us?"

"That, too."

He considers me. Runs a finger down my cheek. "I fucked you. Hard. And you enjoyed it."

I glare at him. "Is there any law against that?"

A corner of his mouth twitches. There's a dark light in his pale eyes as he rises and gives me a hand up. "You are fairly... unexpected in many ways, too, Wendy Darling."

"Says the man with the two faces." I instinctively put my hands over my breasts but he grabs them and pulls them down, his hungry gaze roving over my naked, marked body. "How did you wrestle your Shadow under control? I thought you'd leave me here, tied up, and be on your way, and I..." My voice wobbles and I swallow hard, annoyed at myself.

He releases my hands and swipes his thumb under my eyes. "You cried," he whispers. "I caused you pain."

"Yeah."

His shadow shivers behind him, rises, twists his face—and with a curse, he takes a step back. "You're dangerous, Wendy."

"Dangerous? That's funny. You're the one with the hungry, sadistic shadow."

"It wants you." He shakes his head. "I want you, so it wants you, too."

It's my turn to blink at him and stare. The way he said it, the way he breathed that word—"want"—it felt as if he was still inside of me. It felt like something more.

Especially when he shrugs out of his shirt and drapes it over me, his gaze darkening.

Gathering myself together, pulling on the shirt that smells of him and taking a few twigs out of my tangled hair, I take a breath. "Jas. This is important. I know you said no, but I really, really need you to send me back to the human world. I won't stay and take everyone down with me."

"Peter wants to save you," Jas says quietly, that low growl still in his voice. "You and your world."

"I don't care, I... I can't..."

"You do care. You have family there, don't you?"

"I do." I swallow hard. "My brothers. My friend Charlie is like family, too."

"And your parents."

I frown. "Right…"

"And you are still very young. We have lived a very long time, Wendy, and maybe… maybe he's right and it's for the best. We are all tired."

"What? No. You can't give up. There has to be a way, right? A way to save the island, save all of you?"

"No, Wendy—"

"There has to be. It's why you were looking for me."

"*Peter* was looking for you," Jas says, folding his arms over his muscular chest and I try not to stare at the scar. "Not me."

"And you didn't want me to come. You tried to stop him again and again, because… because you knew this might happen. That if he found me and if I started facing my fears, the island would crumble. But then how? How did Peter expect me to save you?"

"I don't think he even has the answer to that himself. He probably thought that if you faced your fears, your past, you could fix this, fix the island, fix the bridge, but so far this endeavor seems to be having the opposite effect. You can't fix it, so it will have to sink. I suppose… it could have gone either way."

"But I have barely started remembering the past, barely scratched the surface. What if there is still hope?"

"Then you'd better do it quickly," Jas says, "and find out. In any case, a quick end is better than a drawn-out one."

"Don't say that," I whisper.

"Facing your fears means facing the truth. The truth always hurts."

"But it also heals," I say.

"So they say. I'm not sure about that myself. Sending you back will only delay the inevitable. I suppose there could be another Wendy. Another attempt. But there isn't time. The Night of Nights is coming. And then it's all over, at last."

"Sounds ominous," I say past a lump of fear in my throat. "So what will it be, Jas? Will you send me back, save the island, save your friends?"

"Who says they are my friends?"

"I understand they used to be. And you'd like them to be again."

"Bullshit," he breathes but there is no heat in the word.

"Is it?"

"Yeah. I'm taking you back to Peter Pan."

"Jas, no. Wait." I resist when he grabs my arm and hauls me down a trail. "Please. Please, send me back to the human world, please don't let this—"

The soldiers suddenly surround us, lifting dully glinting black swords.

"What's happening?" Jas pulls me against his side and I slam against warm skin. One of the soldiers throws him his own sword, the blade a blinding silver and white. He lifts it and it burns like a beacon—the weapons of a champion in shiny armor with angels at his back, not of a dark knight with an army of ghosts surrounding him.

And then I see it.

It's as if the woods have been splashed with blood, red all around us, scarlet limbs and big badass guns and grinning-skull red faces, towering all around us.

Reds.

"How the fuck did they get the drop on us?" Jas hisses.

I lift my hands. "Maybe they snuck while you were fucking me?"

He snorts. "Not funny."

Yeah, it isn't. We're about to die, because no matter how good Jas' ghost soldiers are, the Reds are bigger, with guns, and seem to fill the woods like a crimson plague.

"Who do they answer to, anyway?" I wonder. "Why do they keep attacking?"

"They belong to the island," Jas says. "They are its guardians, made from its soil. They know your purpose is to sink the island, so their goal is to end you."

"Oh, great. What if I tell them I don't want to sink the island? Do they even speak English, or…" I trail off, staring at the Reds, shock racing through me. "Wait a minute. Their faces. They've changed again."

"Have they?"

"Yeah, now they have a male face and…" And it's somehow familiar. Very familiar. "Oh, holy crap, don't tell me…"

No more time to wallow in shock. The Reds attack, a rushing ruby tide, and Jas hauls me behind him. Then turning, he manages to lift me over his shoulder and start running.

Whoa. By the time I realize it, we're pounding away in the other direction, leaving the shadow soldiers fighting the Reds behind us. But before we go far, we hear running steps and then come face to face with none other than Peter and the Lost Boys.

"Wendy!" Peter cries out. "Jas."

"Put me down." I slam my fists in the small of Jas's back and unexpectedly he does put me down, letting me slide off his shoulder to the ground.

There they are, Peter and Tink and the Twins, and it warms my chest to see them.

But there is no time.

"Come on, this way," Tink says, taking my hand and pointing toward what looks like a cluster of pines. "Hurry!"

"Wendy!" Wes glances at me as we race away. "We were looking for you. You were… with Jas?"

"Long story," I whisper, my face heating.

"The Reds' faces have changed again," he says. "Now they have a male face—?"

"My dad."

"What did he do?" He slows down, two bright spots on his

cheekbones. "Wendy... when you said your mom was jealous of the attention he paid you... holy shit, is it what I think it was?"

"No. No." I'm shaking my head even as Peter catches my wrist and we all come to a halt. "No, Wes."

Tink's hold on my hand tightens. I'm caught between him and Peter. "What did your father do, Wendy? What did he do to you?"

"Did he touch you in ways and places he shouldn't?" Colt asks, his dark eyes blazing. "Did he abuse you, Wendy? It's a simple question."

"But maybe there isn't a simple answer!" I yell at him, feeling like I'm going to puke and explode at the same time. Scaredy-cat-explode.

Because I don't remember. I don't want to remember.

"Dee," Peter starts, and I don't want to hear it.

"The only thing that matters," I say, interrupting him, "is that I have to go back to my world. I can't sink this island. I won't."

"Wendy, no." Wes gives me this serious look that is so cute. "You can't go back. Not before shattering the bridge. Then Jas will send you back, of course he will, but this is important. You have to do it."

"Is it because you don't want to face your fears?" Tink mutters.

"Like *you* have?" I shoot back and he blanches. "Shit. Tink..."

"No, I deserved that," he says, his cheeks pale.

Maybe he's right. But maybe there is a reason I don't want to face my fears and it doesn't have to do with the island.

It has to do with my sanity.

"Guys, shut your pieholes." Peter frowns, tilts his head—in much the same way Jas had done when listening to his shadow.

"What is it?" I whisper.

"The Reds. We should haul ass, now."

22

WENDY

Running doesn't provide the best conditions for discussion, so as we race among trees and brambles, I swallow my questions and fears, try to suppress once more the memories bubbling to the surface.

It doesn't help, either, that at some point Peter picks me up bodily, since I'm apparently slowing us down, and swings me up in his arms.

No matter how secure his hold, being held by a running man means a lot of rocking and thumping against a solid chest, no matter how hard I grip his neck.

Yeah, no talking in the cards right now.

But the memories keep rising like bubbles in a swamp, awful and stinky and unwelcome. They flash through my mind, forcing me to look, really look and recall.

My parents fighting.

Doors being slammed, furniture crashing through the house.

Screaming and yelling.

My brothers cowering under the table, staring at me with round eyes.

"My mom was jealous of me, because my dad paid me too much attention."

Dad, swinging me up in his arms, whirling me around. Bringing home dresses for me. Shoes. Jewelry. Combing my hair at night. Stroking my face. Having me stroke his cheeks.

Mom, watching from the door of the bedroom. Mom, her eyes wild, full of anger and hurt.

Dad, asking me to come into the room with him, or the bathroom. Undressing me. Telling me how pretty I am.

Mom, screaming her head off at Dad and me. Mom saying she'd end it all.

And the boat. All of us sitting on the benches, a picnic basket at our feet, Dad rowing, then Mom yelling at him, pointing at me.

Cold sweat running down my back, between my breasts, into my eyes, stinging, burning.

My mouth dry, my heart thumping in my ears...

"Wendy!" someone says. "She's remembering something, I just know it. Wendy, what did you remember?"

...Mom slapping Dad, screaming at him, pointing at me again, calling me a slut and a whore and a freak degenerate, and I don't know what she's talking about, only that she's mad, mad at me, mad, so frigging mad, she's at the end of her tether and about to do something drastic.

Something terrible.

When she grabs me and shoves me overboard, I don't even make a sound. The cold water hits my face, gets into my eyes, my mouth, my nose. Salty water, stinging like my sweat, and I gulp, trying to get air, but all I get is water.

Of course, I don't know how to swim. We'd never lived near the ocean or any body of water. My parents never sent us to the pool for swimming lessons.

I go under.

Into darkness.

Blue shapes that seem to move.

Ripples of light.

Hands reach for me, dragging me down, dragging me deeper, when I start to finally struggle, running out of air, starting to panic. Suffocating. Drowning.

I don't want to die!

Please, I don't want to d—

"Wendy! Breathe for me! Breathe, you're okay, come on, you can do it!" Hands are shaking me, and something about the voice, the hands themselves, the urgency, it makes me draw in air.

And start coughing.

"Good girl, good girl!" The hands are now patting my back. "This is it. You can do it."

I blink up at Peter, and Tink, and... everyone.

I'm not in the sea, not in the past, not drowning. I almost smile in relief. I'm okay, all is good, I'm safe—

Wait. Wasn't I being carried in Peter's arms as we ran away from... "The Reds!" I gasp, trying to sit up.

"We lost them," Colt says, dark eyes glittering. "At least, I think we did. Are you okay?"

"What happened?" I whisper.

"You started gasping, like you couldn't breathe," Tink says, green eyes wide. "We were worried."

"We want to know you are okay," Wes says.

"So now you care about me and want me safe?" Irrational anger rises in me, feeding on my fear and panic. "After using me for sexual relief? After forcing me to face my greatest fears?"

Colt shrugs and looks away.

Wes rubs the back of his head.

Peter growls something I can't make out.

Tink's cheekbones turn pink.

And Jas snorts softly.

My eyes feel hot. *Oh, God.* Is it true? Do they really care? They haven't denied it. But do they mean it? Can you contrive such reactions? Am I misreading them?

"What did you see?" Peter asks and he has to clear his voice before going on, "What did you recall?"

I swallow hard, still feeling the salt scraping my throat raw, the water filling my lungs. "She pushed me. *Mom.* Into the sea. She was angry because Dad... Dad touched me as he should be touching her."

"Ah, fuck, Wendy..." Peter's face twists, and then, unexpectedly, he draws me into his arms, cradles me against his chest. Rocks me. "I'm so fucking sorry."

"It's..." I can't say it's okay, because it's not, it's fucked up, but telling them about my memories, speaking the words out loud feels... liberating. I let out a long breath because it's a damn relief.

And then the island collapses.

———

THE EARTH IS SHAKING.

Rocks roll by, crashing into the sea below. In the deafening din of soil, trees and buildings collapsing into the ocean, I think I hear wild laughter.

And then the ground under our feet starts giving away.

"Colt!" I grab for him when he stumbles backward, eyes wide, just managing to stop him from tumbling over the edge of the cliff that has just formed behind him.

The rocks are still crashing down, into the waves.

The sea roars. It's an angry, vicious sound.

A cry rings out and I turn just in time to see Wes falling, arms windmilling, face white. My breath going out of me, I make an abortive movement toward him, Peter, too, but it's too late.

And then Tink falls, the ground where he's standing giving way, a flash of wide eyes and an arching body, and he's gone.

"No!" I yell, this time finding my voice. "Don't—be careful —watch out—!"

Peter stumbles and Colt wrenches away from me to catch him, cursing under his breath, reaches for him—too late, too frigging late as Peter tumbles into the sea in eerie silence, his body seeming to hover in mid-air before plunging down.

Before I know how to react, Colt staggers, and then more of the land collapses, taking him down.

Gasping, I fall to my knees.

No. Please, no.

I can't draw breath. I feel like I'm drowning all over again.

Maybe I was never rescued.

Maybe all this never happened and I'm still at the bottom of the sea, dying.

"Wendy! Wendy, get up. We have to move." Someone has a hold on me, pulling me up. I reel where I stand. My knees are like water, my vision murky and dim. I can't get my feet under me—and what's the use in murky water?—but he's relentless and damn strong because he hauls me up, and then higher up. I'm in his arms, pressed to his bare chest, I realize but the knowledge is distant and useless. "We have to go before the rest of the island sinks."

It's a while before my senses come back, but I'm already fighting his hold.

"Put me down," I breathe, trying to shove him away, trying to get free, then blink until the dark haze clears and I make out trees and rocks. "Where are we? I thought you said the island would sink."

"Most of it. This is the last part left out of the water. The Hill."

"I've never been here," I whisper.

"No. You haven't."

"Jas—"

"I'll send you home," Jas says, "like Peter wanted."

"No. No!" I struggle against him. "You can't! Don't send me back now. We have to go get them. Save them!"

"You want to dive into the sea that is the source of your nightmares?" Jas chuckles, a dry, bitter sound. "Yeah, right. So long, Wendy Darling. You didn't save the worlds, the island or us. So it was meant to be."

"No, no, no..."

"Let me tell you this: for this rock to be still standing, you haven't faced all your fears. What else do you still have buried inside that blond head of yours?" He tilts his head to the side, gazing down at me, his pale hair fluttering, his arms secure around me. "One last memory."

I shiver. He won't let me fall.

I have to let go and dive deep on my own. That's what he wants, what he's asking of me and I can't... I can't.

He finally sets me down on my feet but he takes my hand, pulling me to him. "What is it, girl? What else are you hiding from yourself? Might as well reach the end of your tether, open your arms and let yourself fall. My friends..." He snarls. "They are already gone. What else are you keeping back?"

"Please, Jas—" I manage to snag my hand away, rubbing at it. "Stop."

"You know," he grinds out, "Peter was never the brightest bulb, but he was right about this, I reckon. It's for the best. Let this cursed island and its haunted inhabitants vanish forever."

"Don't say that!" The grief hits me like a punch to the chest. I'm gasping again, unable to deal with this blow. "Don't ever say this. I can't..."

"It's done, Wendy. They're dead. And..." He rakes his hand through his silvery hair, nods, brows pulled over his eyes. "And I'll follow them soon."

"Jas, no..."

He takes out his crocodile-skin pocket watch from the pocket of his pants and frowns down at it. Then he smirks a little as he pulls back his arm and throws it into the waves. His gaze is all stars and comets, blinding and bright as it vanishes in the heaving sea. "It's been a pleasure meeting you, Wendy Darling."

I shake my head, take a step back. "Jas—"

"This is goodbye."

His face blinks out, the island around me vanishes, and I fall—like Peter and the Lost Boys had. Arms windmilling, body arching, eyes wide...

And land on a bed without a sound, inside a familiar room.

Golden light is seeping through the window.

My books are on the shelf.

And Charlie's voice rings out in the next room, saying something about bills and salaries and fate.

I'm home.

Burying my face in the pillow, I cry.

———

"You were asleep when I got back in the afternoon," Charlie says later as I sit across from her at our tiny kitchen table. She sounds baffled. Looks baffled. Her eyebrows haven't come down from her forehead since I walked into her room, still crying, and I wonder if they'll stay that way from now on. "I thought maybe you were sleeping off a cold or something. I don't normally find you asleep in bed when I come home. It's pretty early for bedtime but you were out like a light."

"But..." I rub my aching head. "But I was gone, I was on the island..."

"What island?"

"Neverland. Peter..." Already the memories of the island seem distant and fogged over. Like an old movie, like a sequence of faded photographs. "Peter Pan and the Lost Boys. Tink, Colt, Wes... And Hook."

She gives me an uncertain smile. "Sounds like a fairytale. Or a dream."

"It was neither. It was real. I am..." I swear I still feel the bruises they left on my body, inside of me when they had sex with me, I feel the imprint of their fingers on my wrists, my forearms, my hips, my neck. I can almost feel cum running down my thighs.

But there is nothing. I checked when I found myself back here. No evidence.

Am I going crazy? Is this what this is? Is the past catching up with me? Will it land me in an asylum after all?

"Dee? What's wrong? You got that weird look on your face and you have gone all pale. Are you sick?"

"I don't know," I whisper. "Maybe I am."

"Aw. What's wrong, girl?" Charlie gets up, comes around the table and leans over me, opening her arms. "Give us a hug."

Grateful, I let her pull me into her arms, squashing our boobs together.

She smells familiar and sweet. She's my friend.

I'm home.

Then why doesn't it feel like it's enough? Why doesn't Charlie's presence and her warm hug comfort me?

Why do I miss those asshole boys so much? It's like they carved up a place in my heart, with their mystery and their small vulnerable moments and their godawful behavior, the rough sex and manhandling, but also their protectiveness, and...

And it makes no sense. I barely know them. And guys like that I should put in my rear-view mirror.

I know that.

Wendy knows that. The rational, goal-oriented Wendy I

was what feels like yesterday knows that, but now my head is full of new memories, and old ones, too.

Faint as they are, they persist.

Frowning to myself, I get up and pace to the window. I have this weird memory that I've stood here before, watching... Peter... and then I went to Neverland to find him.

What do I want? My goal all these years was to leave home, find a job, save money, bring my brothers here.

No matter what my parents did to me... it never seemed to affect them. Never touched them—and even as my mind shies away from what my parents did, still I know I need to get them out of there.

Because you never know. Unhinged people are, after all, unhinged and could hurt them.

What that makes me, then? Me with my undeniable attraction to the psychos of the island? It's not the rough sex I'm thinking about, but their general craziness, and...

Yeah. I'm probably unhinged, too.

It doesn't matter, though, does it? What I want, what I really want, what tugs on my heart and occupies my mind, is the boys falling into the sea.

Did that happen?

Was it real?

Are they all dead?

A sob catches in my throat, and I press a hand to my mouth to stifle it before Charlie comes over to investigate. She knew I was crying earlier. Impossible to hide it from her.

I wish I could go back to the island, just in case... just in the unlikely case the boys are still alive, that I can save them. After all, they are magical. Would the mermaids eat them? Or keep their bodies as trophies? I doubt they'd make a boat for them to live on, that would be...

...impossible.

The thought comes to a screeching halt when the man

standing on the street below my window glances up. Caught in the pool of light cast by the street lamp, he looks familiar.

The light glints silver on his tousled hair.

In his gray eyes.

His crooked grin.

I press my hand to the glass, astonished. "*Jas?*"

> "Time is chasing after all of us."
> — J.M. Barrie, Peter Pan

QUEEN OF DREAMS (BRUTAL NEVER BOYS 3)

Coming June 21!

What makes us go back to our fears and dark desires, again and again, unable to escape?

I thought it was all over. That I was back in the human world, for good this time. Back in my apartment, with my friends, my job, my life.

But the heart works in mysterious ways and it won't let me rest. When I find out that the Lost Boys might still be alive, I jump at the chance to go back to the island and save them.

Losing them would be unbearable, even though I ran away from them once before.

Only problem is, saving them means I'll have to face my greatest fear, plunge into the unknown and accept what I did and who I am.

Can I do it?

Will it work?

And even if I manage... where do we go from there? Will love prove strong enough to save us all?

OTHER BOOKS FROM MONA BLACK!

Book 1 in the Cursed Fae Kings series (standalone fae romance novels series):
<u>The Merman King's Bride</u>
A cursed King of Faerie
A princess betrothed to a man she doesn't love
A kiss that will change everything

The last thing Princess Selina expects to find in the lake in the woods is a handsome merman. His name is Adar and he saves her, teases her, kisses her, and tells her she could break his curse.

Because, as it turns out, he's a Fae King, cursed to remain in merman form until he finds a princess to kiss him.

But one kiss is not enough and Selina has other problems.

Such getting engaged to a prince she isn't sure she even likes, let alone loves. Marrying him and having his children is not on her list of favorite things.

And now she's falling for the merman.

He's everything she could wish for in a man. Handsome, protective, kind. Except that he is Fae. And has a fishtail.

Still, she can't stop thinking about him. Keeps going back to him. Craves his kisses.

Would gladly have his babies.

Is this a spell, or is it love? Can she break the curse and save Adar? Will there be a happy ending to their story?

All a girl can do is try. After all, true love is worth fighting for and Selina knows she has found it.

This book is standalone novella-length NA romance fantasy novel, featuring mature situations with some dark themes and adult language. It is a retelling of the Frog Prince, with all the emotions, romance, spice and heat.

———

A completed Paranormal Reverse Harem series! Welcome to Pandemonium Academy!

<u>**"Of Boys and Beasts"**</u>

One's a werewolf with an ax to grind

Two's a vampire with a heart of coal

Three's a demon with a taste for pain

Four's a fae with a past of woe

Five's a girl who will take them down all

In revenge for the pain they've sown

So what if they're gorgeous? They must atone...

My name is Mia Solace. You know, the girl who will take them down all? That's me.

When my cousin is returned to us by Pandemonium Academy in a glass coffin, in an enchanted sleep she isn't expected to wake up from, I grab her diary and head to the academy myself.

Because her diary, you see, tells of four cruel boys who

bullied her and broke her heart until she sought oblivion through a spell.

Four magical boys, because that's the world we live in now, heirs of powerful families attending this elite academy where the privileged scions of the human and magical races are brought together in the noble pursuit of education.

As for me, I cheat to get on the student roster, and once I'm in, well… it's war, baby. I'll get those four sons of guns, steal their secrets, make them hurt. I'll transform into an avenging angel for my cousin, for all the girls they've wronged, and I bet there are plenty of those.

While growing up, my cousin was my only friend. Now I'll be her champion.

Only these boys aren't exactly as I pictured them. Devastatingly handsome, deliciously brooding, strangely haunted, they're getting under my skin and through my defenses.

Kissing them surely wasn't part of my plan…

Getting into bed with them even less.

ABOUT MONA BLACK

Mona is a changeling living in the human world. She writes fantasy romance and reverse harem romance, and is an avid reader of fantasy and paranormal books. One day she will get her ducks in a row and get a cat so she can become a real author.

Check out her paranormal reverse harem series Pandemonium Academy Royals, and her fantasy romance series Cursed Fae Kings.

Books by Mona

Fairytale Retellings
The Merman King's Bride (Cursed Fae Kings 1)
The Beast King's Bride (Cursed Fae Kings 2)
The Feral King's Bride (Cursed Fae Kings 3)

Paranormal Reverse Harem
FREE Prequel to of Boys and Beasts - Of Girls and Stories
Of Boys and Beasts (Pandemonium Academy Royals 1)

Of Beasts and Demons (Pandemonium Academy Royals 2)
Of Demons and Witches (Pandemonium Academy Royals 3)
Of Witches and Queens (Pandemonium Academy Royals 4)